The Lighting of the Lamps

By the same author

The Albatross
The Bird of Night
A Bit of Singing and Dancing
A Change for the Better
Gentleman and Ladies
I'm the King of the Castle
In the Springtime of the Year
Strange Meeting
The Magic Apple Tree
The Woman in Black
Through the Kitchen Window
Through the Garden Gate

Books for Children
One Night at a Time
Mother's Magic

SUSAN HILL

The Lighting of the Lamps

Hamish Hamilton: London

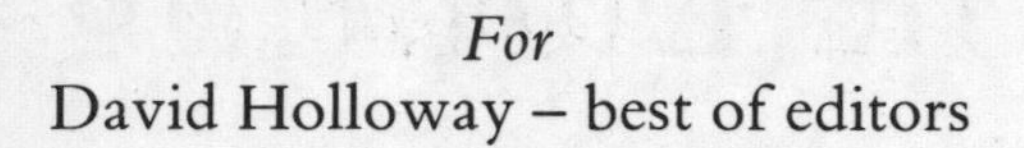

For
David Holloway – best of editors

First published in Great Britain 1987
by Hamish Hamilton Ltd
27 Wrights Lane London W8 5TZ

ISBN 0-241-11985 5

Photoset by Rowland Phototypesetting Ltd
Bury St Edmunds, Suffolk
Printed in Great Britain by
Butler and Tanner Ltd, Frome, Somerset

Contents

Introduction

According to my mother, my first and regularly repeated sentence at the age of less than two, was 'Read-a-book, read-a-book'. And although the anecdote caused me embarrassment when growing up, I have never seen any reason to doubt the truth of it. For my earliest memories are of books and reading, and although I certainly did play with the limited selection of toys available to a war-time child I much preferred either reading books, or inventing imaginary people and conversations and listening to those of adults. A great many of my early memories are of walks, through and about the seaside town of Scarborough in which I was born and spent my entire childhood and adolescence; we walked on the cliffs and along the seashore, along the promenades and through the public gardens, and over the suspension bridges; we walked to school and to the shops and to the library and on visits to my mother's friends, we walked in winter and summer, through wind, snow, rain and gale, of which there was much, and the occasional heatwave. We walked early in the morning and in the long late afternoons and evenings of early dark and, while walking, I looked, and listened, and above all I thought.

All of these things went towards making me into both writer and reader. There were other factors too: the fact that I was an only child of older parents and left to my own devices and in my own company for considerable periods; that there were not many children of my own age living near to us, in the years before adolescence – so that, when I was not at school, I was either alone or with adults; that Scarborough is a dramatic town, both scenically and climatically, and that the war and immediate post-war years were unusually atmospheric ones; that, in those days, the town was full of interesting-looking old ladies, the genteel retired, and, in summer only, interesting crowds of 'trippers', at all of whom I stared, to all of whom I listened intently. Time, solitude, the odd, the adult, the dramatic, the idiosyncratic – the combination was a potent one.

My mother, who brought me up more or less single-handed, had left school at the age of fourteen. She was an immensely practical woman, a dress-designer and a seamstress of considerable skill, with her own small business, a bustling, energetic little woman and no dreamer, but she *was* a reader, a tremendous enjoyer of books both serious and popular, and a believer in education for women, with a passionate ambition for me to go further than she had: to pass examinations, be studious, aim for university.

So the fact that I was surrounded by books and spoke so enthusiastically about them so early was a result of her encouragement as well as of those particular circumstances.

Every Saturday, from the days when I was in a pram, we went to two libraries, the public library and the private, circulating one. I remember being given picture books to look at and then toddling, rather unsteadily, across the highly polished parquet floors between the tall book-stacks and only being able to reach the bottom shelves when I stood on a stool. Whenever I step inside a library, the smell of the place catapults me back to those childhood Saturdays and if I close my eyes I can still walk confidently into every room of that library building as it used to be, the children's library, the entrance hall, with its display cases of new titles, the reference library, silent except for the squeak of a chair leg, the soft turn of a page – the periodicals room, where old men coughed over newspapers, the stairs leading to the upper halls where I wandered around exhibitions of amateur photography and water-colour societies and in which, in the 1950s, Stephen Joseph started his celebrated theatre-in-the-round, the forerunner of the Library Theatre that nurtured Alan Ayckbourn. Buildings have always been extremely important to me and those like the Scarborough Public Library, in which I spent so much time, became as familiar as home, and I felt at home within them. I was perfectly happy and perfectly safe left to my own devices in the separate, flat-roofed building which housed the children's library, and it was there that I learned to choose for myself – an essential lesson and one which requires a good deal of practice – as I realised when my own elder daughter acquired library tickets of her own. Because we live in the country, at some distance from the public library, and because there have always been a great number of books in the house – bought copies, complimentary copies, review copies, gifts – she had not, until the age of about eight, been a regular library borrower, as I was, and so, when faced with the wide array of children's books in the nearest branch library, she became totally confused and bemused, and in the end would grab a handful of anything, regardless of whether it was aimed roughly at her own age group or children of four years younger or six years older, was fiction or non-fiction, or even whether she had read it before. The answer to the problem was simply regular and frequent library visits, a little but not too much parental assistance, trial and error and ample time – all of which were granted to me in abundance.

On Saturday morning we went to the public library, but in the afternoon we went to the other end of the town and to a small private, circulating library, of which there were very many in the years before and immediately after the War. It was in two rooms of a house in the middle of a shopping parade and, unlike the public library, frequented almost entirely by women – middle-aged and middle-class. Its stock, to which the newest titles were regularly added, consisted mainly of fiction and good biographies. Authors like Frances Parkinson Keyes, Naomi Jacob, Stella Gibbons, Margaret Kennedy, Neville Shute, Georgette Heyer, Storm Jameson and dozens of others now quite forgotten, these formed my mother's staple reading diet. And, if I did not have anything of my own to read on library visits, I would pick one of them off the shelves and read a page or two myself, and be granted glimpses into colourful, strange adult worlds of which I understood little but which fascinated and tantalized me.

In an absorbing book, *A Very Great Profession,** Nicola Beauman presents a study of the woman's novel from 1914 to 1939 of exactly this kind, and in it she has a quotation from Jan Struther's famous novel *Mrs. Miniver* which evokes for me a

* (Virago, London 1983)

whole era of my childhood and afternoons and early evenings spent with my mother on opposite chairs reading, reading.

'Tea was already laid: there were honey sandwiches, brandy snaps, small ratafia biscuits: and there would, she knew, be crumpets. Three new library books lay virginally on the fender-stool, their bright paper wrappers unsullied by subscriber's hand. The clock on the mantelpiece chimed, very softly and precisely, five times.'

Indeed the reading of books when young is associated altogether with certain times, certain places: reading lying on my stomach under a hawthorn tree whose pungent blossom was one of the pervading scents of childhood – now and again a spider or a ladybird would crawl across the pages of my book, or a fragment of the creamy-white blossom would fall into it; reading in a hump under the bedclothes, by the light of a very weak torch; reading in the hayloft above a riding stable on an aunt's farm, and deep in a red armchair on winter afternoons with the north-easterly gale howling outside, battering the windows and roaring like a beast down the chimney. I was a highly omnivorous reader from the age of about four, when I was first able to cope with print unaided, although there were certain kinds of book which left me cold and continue to do so; I had never any interest in historical fiction and have none now nor indeed any very strong historical sense at all, except of a personal nature, I tried Arthur Ransome several times and always failed to enter into the spirit of his children's adventures; stories with animals as heroes were never much read, nor did I care for witches, wizards, the other worlds of gnomes or fairies, or any form of science fiction. Quite why all of these books did not involve my imagination I do not know – taste in literature is a curious thing, as curious as taste in food, and the depths of an individual's inner life to which writers lay siege are unfathomable.

Looking back, I find it equally odd and inexplicable that I had a passion for non-fiction books of travel, adventure and exploration, for *The Kon Tiki Expedition* and Arthur Grimble's *A Pattern of Islands* and in particular, beginning with *The Ascent of Everest*, for anything at all about the Antarctic. I read avidly about whaling boats and about explorers like Magellan and Christopher Columbus, about the road to

Samarkand and the desert nomads, Australian aborigines and the rain forests of South America, I, who had never travelled outside Europe and not very widely within it, and who, as I grow older, grow ever more reluctant to stir from my own fireside, I am and always was the archetypal armchair traveller.

Let it not be thought that all my reading was edifying, nourishing and wholesome. I read my way through Enid Blyton and pony books, ballet books, comics, any old stuff, learning in the process to sort the wheat from the chaff. I am still a great believer in the therapeutic value of an occasional dose of frivolity, nonsense, and downright rubbish, so long as it is morally harmless rubbish. Once, like my daughter, I escaped into *The Beano*, now it is into glossy magazine.

But it was fiction which claimed me first and last. And there were certain books which became so much part of me, that I knew their chapters by heart and inhabited the landscapes in my waking and sleeping dreams. Above all, and first of all, there was *Alice in Wonderland* and *Alice Through the Looking Glass*. I find it hard to separate what was real in my childhood from what belonged to the world of Alice, so closely did Lewis Carroll's vision interweave my imagination. The rabbit hole, the garden of live flowers, the croquet match, the looking glass drawing-room, the chequerboard fields across which ran and jumped the little train, these were mine, I walked about in those places and talked with those people, I *was* Alice. I cannot now look at a pack of playing cards without a feeling of affection for these old particular friends.

Everyone who reads early, and reads with absorption, has such key books which are far more than books to them and become part of their inner lives for ever after, though the reason why it should be book X rather than book Y is another mystery. Chance plays a part, chance and serendipity, but there must be more to this affinity, this intimate link between person and book, readers and writers, creative spirits, even though any attempt at detailed analysis and explanation is as unwise and unnecessary as an analysis of what makes this person fall in love with that.

From the beginning, I was allowed access to adult bookshelves and there discovered, long before I was officially old enough for them, *Wuthering Heights* and *Jane Eyre*, *Vanity Fair* and *Kidnapped*, *A Pilgrim's Progress* and *The Mill on the Floss*, all of which puzzled, fascinated, inspired and terrified me by turns. But no other author, apart from Lewis Carroll, took me by the scruff of the neck and held me – and has held me ever since – until, at the age of nine, I was given a complete set of the novels of Charles Dickens. I have that edition still, it is the one I would always prefer to read from, though the print is very small and rather poor, and the pages yellowing, and reading an entire novel is very trying on the eyes. Never mind. It is a sentimental matter of familiarity, fondness for the blurred words and the musty smell and the brown leatherette jackets, which are bound up for me so closely with the contents of the volumes. Dickens fired my imagination, excited it and stirred it, coloured it in the most vivid and powerfully dramatic way. Whole scenes of his are permanently engraved on my mind, like a series of tableaux or illustrated animated pictures: the graveyard and Miss Haversham's room in *Great Expectations*, the charnel-house and Tom-All-Alone's in *Our Mutual Friend,* Little Dorrit's prison, the screaming crowds waiting for the execution in *A Tale of Two Cities*, the burning buildings in *Barnaby Rudge*. I read for hour upon hour, lost to myself and my own surroundings, deaf to all voices except those from the world of the book. I can remember coming to, at the end of reading *David Copperfield*, and wondering where I was, feeling unreal and lost and wanting to dive back inside the story, as I wanted so desperately to find a way of crawling down the little passage that led to the beautiful garden where Alice longed to walk 'among those beds of bright flowers and those cool fountains'.

The power of great imaginative literature, the longings and desires it awakens, are stronger than any save those of love. That my parents were never critical, resentful or suspicious of the influence books had over me is to their everlasting credit, for there certainly is the opposite, Gradgrind school of thought which holds that such passionate commitment to fiction is dangerous escapism, detrimental to the acquisition of useful learning, real relationships and physical development. Too much reading inflames the brain, so we were told, and that I could believe, there were times when my own *did* seem to be on fire with what had so absorbed and excited me, but it is to such delight and such pain and to those hours in which one is transported out of oneself to other worlds that both serious reader and writer too owe so much, without them a full and true understanding of literature can never be attained.

Books, the reading and subsequently the writing of them, have always dominated my life and it seemed self-evident both to me and to my teachers that I would aim to read English Literature at University – what else *could* I have read? But again there was another school of thought, which I encountered then and have argued passionately against since, which held that anyone proposing to be a writer and particularly a novelist should steer clear of studying the subject as an academic one but instead do history or modern languages or classics – almost anything. Quite apart from the fact that I had no aptitude for or interest in those subjects, I was as baffled at the age of eighteen as I still am now by the advice. What better way of preparing to be a writer than by spending three years immersed in the work of the greatest novelists, poets, dramatists, essayists in the English language – not in order to imitate, but to absorb and be inspired by? If I had not been required to do so I doubt if I would ever have studied so much English literature so systematically and thoroughly, and learned, by the training of my own critical faculties, to analyse and appreciate. I would certainly have gone on reading, where my own fancy led me, but the self-discipline, not to mention time and facilities, required for covering an enormous amount of ground, from Anglo-Saxon and medieval English, through the eighteenth and nineteenth centuries to Eliot, Auden, and beyond, would have been altogether lacking. I read things in my three years at the University of London that I might never have come across for myself and without immediate and obvious appeal, and reading the literary criticism of them, together with having to do my own, did nothing but enhance and deepen my understanding. Nor did any of it deaden my enthusiasm for writing myself. I published my first novel, written while in the sixth form, the term I arrived at University, and the second just before I took Finals. That neither was any good is beside the point.

It was at University too that I began writing book reviews,

simply because I was asked to do so. David Pryce-Jones, then Literary Editor of *Time and Tide*, had written about my own first novel himself and got in touch with me to offer me my first batch of new books for review. The system whereby very young novelists, barely through the starting gate on a writer's career, immediately begin to criticize the work of others is one that still prevails in literary journalism and may not be altogether fair on the authors at the receiving end of some very green judgements; but to be plunged in at the deep end, given six books to be read and pronounced upon pithily in six hundred words by a week on Friday is the best possible training for the fledgling critic.

I wrote those first reviews in 1961 and over the course of the next twenty-five years I wrote hundreds of such columns, for a variety of papers, magazines and literary journals. Weekly or monthly book reviewing is in some ways a professional chore but it was the only way in my early years as a writer that I could earn a modest living. Now I do not have to do it for money but I still do it for pleasure, because the arrival of the latest pile of books, smelling of paper, print and packing, never fails to interest and excite me, and although great novels are very rare and even though for every good one I read a score that are very, very bad, I have never lost my enthusiasm for new writers and their work, or my enjoyment in recommending good books to others. For that, I now know, is what reviewing is or should be all about. I have never seen myself as an academic literary critic, though I am grateful that I had my basic training as one. My aim in every introduction, every 'World of Books' column, every review, every broadcast is to impart the flavour and quality of books that I have enjoyed and admired and which have meant something important to me. I want to awaken enthusiasm, encourage more reading, I am, I suppose, a literary evangelist, rather than a critic, which is not to say I like everything – as I get older I like less and less – but what I do not care for or do not think to be any good, what is pretentious, meretricious, silly, tawdry, badly written or just plain dull, I now can simply ignore.

As a reviewer of new books, of course, one is at the mercy of what is published and sent on to one. When David Holloway offered me my own monthly column in the *Daily Telegraph* I was given the precious freedom to choose my own topic under the general heading of 'The World of Books' and in that space I have been able to write about the books that I have most admired, been influenced, moved and uplifted by, as well as those which have diverted, amused and entertained me throughout my reading life. To share my enthusiasms with others, to try and persuade and cajole them to give this or that a try, to lament the decline of reading time in schools and among adolescents, to welcome and even on occasion instigate reprints of books by long-forgotten writers – this has been the purpose and pleasure of the column. For what I care about most, outside of my family and the landscape of England, is English literature – books, reading, writing, libraries, bookshops, authors, readers. I care that children should not only be taught the mechanics of reading at as early an age as possible but the excitement, mystery, joy, fun, inspiration of reading too, that they should come to be transported and inflamed by books, to learn from them and live inside them, so that literature and the world's writers create become part of their own very fibre and spirit. I do not despise visual aids or the technological revolution for learning purposes and I do not have a mystical attitude to the book as a sacred object. But I do care more than anything that the rising generations should not fail to value and be moulded by great imaginative literature and influenced by the great writers, past, present and future, of the English language. If there is a purpose behind every aspect of my work it is that, to impart to as many other people as possible and particularly to the young something of the pleasure and mystery, magic and strangeness and delight in reading which I discovered as a small child and which has never weakened.

In those childhood days, just as now, when I was not reading I was often to be found listening to the radio, for radio has always seemed to me to be in some way an extension of book reading, it uses the same imaginative faculties, occupies the same quiet and solitary spaces. The writing of radio plays has also been for me all of a piece with the writing of novels and I meant them as much to be read as to be heard. Those included here are, like the pieces selected from over one hundred contributions to 'The World of Books', among those written since 1974 that I wish to be preserved in permanent, printed form.

Reading and writing are very private activities, yet no one spends twenty-five years as a professional woman of letters without the backing of an army of supporters. I owe a debt of gratitude to parents, teachers, editors, publishers, friends, my family. But most of all to that invisible host, the great writers of English literature. To them my debt is inexpressible, to them I shall continue to turn, as I have turned every day for the past forty years, in many moods, many places, at many times, but most of all at the best part of the day, when it is time for 'the lighting of the lamps'.

A Sense of Place

Places. An Anthology of Britain.
Chosen by Ronald Blythe.
(Oxford University Press)

Aldeburgh: the Vision and the Reality

There are two Aldeburghs, and yet they are one. Yet not one. Separate and distinct. The first may belong to anyone; certainly to those who live there, and to its visitors, festival and fishing people and families on holiday, to all who enjoy it for a day or for years, who work and play there. I lived and worked there for spells, made friends, felt both at home and not so, and now, occasionally, and less often than I would like, I go back. I was not born there, I do not belong to the county of Suffolk at all, but much farther up the same coast, in Yorkshire. My ties with Aldeburgh are all of a different order. Yes, there is that real small town, what is left of it after hundreds of years of storm and tide have washed into it and it has crumbled and fallen, so that the Moot Hall is at the very edge, where once it was in the very centre. There is that visible, visitable place; from Liverpool Street to Saxmundham and then take to the road, and there are fast dual carriageways, now, converging upon it from three directions, and the sea at the other door. There are people who live in houses painted fondant Suffolk pink and cream and grey, or else in terraces cut into the hill like tiers of a cake; people who shop for bread and gloves and aspirin, in and out of the long, surprisingly broad High Street, where small shopkeepers still flourish, for this is one of the last places which does not look like every other place.

This is the real town, yes, with the church at the top of the hill and the sea at the bottom and lanes like fingers of a spread hand poking out to reach it here and here and here, so that you only need to follow any one of them along, to fetch out before and beside its great greyness, only need to follow the salt wind in your nostrils and the hiss and boom and suck of it in your ears.

It is a place much favoured by the energetic retired and for holidays by the intellectual middle classes and a place of boats, pleasure boats, leisure boats, and the working fishing boats, dragged up on to the shingle. It is the music town, with a Festival every year since 1948, well known the world over and in summer, thronged with drummers and pluckers, bowers and blowers, a busy town of golf and whist, Red Cross and Royal National Lifeboat Institution.

Yes, all that, and it is indeed real enough and very pleasing.

But for me, there is another Aldeburgh, and perhaps it is not real. It is as though I open a door in my mind, a door that leads into my own past and to parts of my inner self, a place of my own imagination, which I have written about under different guises in different books, and I am still haunted by it, dream of it.

It was Britten, of course, who brought me to Aldeburgh, he was the Pied Piper and I followed his music until I came to it and heard it, at the heart, on the moan of the wind and in the cries of the curlews, in the thunder of the sea, and the stillness of it, too, as the moonlight lay over it on quiet, clear nights. The beach, the marshes, and the names of all the places around and about, and in, and in between, was like a country invented by his genius.

I find it impossible to be detached about Aldeburgh. I could not write of it plainly and baldly for any guide book, as 'short history, principal buildings, climate, special attractions'. For not only did I first come to it already brimming over with emotion about it, a sense of the place and a passion for it ready formed, not only was it even then partly unreal. I also spent much time in it at a particularly crucial highly charged and rare time of my life, so that I know Aldeburgh through my own emotions and my creative imagination, and through each book that I wrote there and which has left its mark upon me. It is the place in which I experienced deep joy and fulfilment and satisfaction, where I worked best of all and most easily and felt free as a bird. I make it sound romantic and unique and significant and so, for me, it was.

Every year I rented a house there from the depths of winter into very early spring, overlooking – almost *in* – the sea. I saw frost on the shingle and it was sometimes so cold I felt I had lost a skin, the wind battered at walls and windows. And there were those beautiful, vibrant days of late February and March, cloudless, cold, which had a piercing clarity in the air, and there seemed to be sky everywhere, pale sky and silver sea, with the land and houses merely a streak between. Larks spiralled up, the sun shone on the river at Slaughden as on a sheet of metal, the reeds and rushes rattled and shook, dry, dry. On such days, I walked inland for miles and saw no one, I made up page after page in my head, absorbed, concentrated, taut, yet seeing things too, waders in the mud, a heron, still as a tree-stump, the individual blades of grass. There was such a spirit in the air of that place, felt, heard, sensed, glimpsed, in the water and the sky and in the cries of birds.

I wrote all morning, looking up to see a fishing boat or the trawlers that sailed slowly in the far distance, and always the sea, moving about within itself, ruminative, grey, blue, violet, silver, it sang in my ears all day, all night.

I tramped the shingle, too, a noisy walk, head down into the screaming wind, and the gulls shrieked and reeled crazily about, and at night, I was sometimes afraid, and pulled the cat up on to my lap for comfort. For I was always alone there, and alone inside myself, too, that kind of life and work is necessarily utterly lonely. I would not have had it otherwise, and alone, you see and know what is hidden and blurred to you in company, you live on a different level, sensations, ideas, truths, the ghosts of the place, rise up and crowd your consciousness. I could never have been as I was, or written just what I did, in any other place in the world.

Then, sometimes, I would open the window wide on early March mornings, and sit with the sun full on my face and laugh to myself, it was so lovely, and then go out for fish, fresh caught, and dip my toes in the icy sea, and run, run over the stones, or throw them, ducks and drakes, or simply stand, watching some ship break the line of the horizon.

I knew, also, extreme, shattering grief there and the

experience, the memory of it, are bound up with my view of the town, too. I remember how I stood and stared, stared down at the sea lapping over one patch of shingle, and could neither believe nor understand the appalling thing that had happened. That day changed my view of the place forever.

Then, I stopped going there to live alone and work. I have visited since, for days and weekends, but when at leisure and accompanied and so it has been the real, outward, everyday Aldeburgh that I have come to, and my presence there has been somehow superficial. Yet the other town is still there. It must be. I would only have to turn a corner and stand alone in wind and rain, to listen, remember.

For the one place I feel warm affection, and friendship, I enjoy it, recommend it, look it up in guide books and history books, I should like my family to remember it as the unspoilt town for happy seaside holidays.

And the other place . . . Ah, that Aldeburgh I hold within me, set as in the amber you may find on the beach there, it is a landscape of the spirit.

(1981)

Introductions

The Secret Garden

by Frances Hodgson Burnett

(Puffin Books)

People often ask writers whether their stories are 'true' or whether it is all made up. I think that, in most cases, the answer is 'both'. But it is rarely that an author describes real events or people absolutely as they were, in every remembered detail, just as painters do not simply copy what they see, exactly as it is and no more. That would be very boring. A writer may base his or her stories on certain real happenings, or include real places and people in among those which are entirely imaginary, but, especially as they so often come from far back in his past and deep down in his memory, these things are altered, transformed by the power of the imagination until they are not at all the same in every detail as they really were.

Why certain things are remembered so vividly, and come to seem so important, and find a place in the books, while others are forgotten, no one can ever fully know, least of all the writer, for it is often the small things – snatches of conversation, a house, a view, a glimpse of a person seen from the window of a flying train – and the feelings they aroused, which stay to haunt a writer. Something that happens years later triggers off the memory again, and he uses it in his work, sometimes many times.

We may enjoy reading biographies of authors. But probably all the important facts about their lives, and truths about what kind of people they were – what was important to them, what they believed in, how they saw the world, and people, why they wrote in the particular way they did – can best be discovered through reading their books. Only after that is it interesting to find out more, and we want to know not out of mere curiosity, but because it may add to our enjoyment and understanding of what they wrote for us. Frances Hodgson Burnett's later life, and the very many books she wrote (mainly for adults, apart from the famous bestseller, *Little Lord Fauntleroy*), are not of so much interest in relation to *The Secret Garden* as is her childhood. That is so often the case. The novelist Graham Greene has said that it is the first twelve years only of any writer's life which are important.

Frances made up stories, and then wrote them down, from a very early age. She was a solitary child, though she had brothers and sisters and got on with them perfectly well. She dreamed and imagined, invented worlds and filled them with people, made up plays using her dolls. Indeed, all her life, things that really happened to her were never ever to seem so richly satisfying, interesting and absorbing as what went on in her own imagination. It was all a little duller, paler, more disappointing, even though she had a far more successful life than might have been predicted from her poor origins; she became a hugely popular author, married and had two sons, and travelled widely.

From the age of four, she read a great deal and for the most part read books which might be thought 'too old' for her – certainly they were not books intended for children; she read the poetry of Wordsworth, and the plays of Shakespeare, the Bible, the novels of Charles Dickens and Sir Walter Scott. And if she did not 'understand' everything in them, it all formed the stuff of her dreams, it excited her and stimulated her to tell her own stories, and much of it made such a deep impression on her that it buried itself deep within her memory; she was formed by books as much as by real life.

The Burnett family was not poor by the standards of the late Victorian age in which Frances grew up; she saw the children of factory-workers eating stale crusts and going out in the snow without shoes or socks. But they were certainly not rich people either, and life was a constant struggle for Frances's mother (her father died when she was five) who was very anxious to preserve an outward appearance of gentility. When Frances was fifteen, the family emigrated to the United States, hoping to start a more prosperous life. That marked the break with childhood, the start of Frances's grown-up life. Her early experiences and memories were all somehow sealed off, like a ship in a bottle – the past could be kept, whole and untouched, to be taken out much later, looked at and relived through the imagination.

All her life, Frances loved and made gardens, but her obsession with hidden, secret gardens, desolate, neglected ones, can be traced back to the very first gardens she knew as a small child in Manchester, one of which (she later wrote, in her autobiography) was overgrown and 'lay behind a little green door in a high wall . . . It had been a garden once, and there were the high brick walls around it and the little door so long unopened, and once there had been flowers and trees in it'. In her mind's eye, she saw it filled again with sunshine and growing, blossoming, fruiting plants, flowers, trees, scented, humming with bees and birds, alive. She was learning how the human imagination could transform reality, make things new, bring them to life.

When she was a middle-aged woman, renting a house in Sussex, all those early memories of gardens were aroused again by a wonderful old secret orchard garden there, surrounded by another high wall, and they came together as she began to create the garden at Misselthwaite. It is, of course, a place of poetry, a symbolic place, where the magic works, first to release Mary Lennox from her loneliness and stiffness, and then to heal and free Colin Craven from all his inner terrors and self-obsessions about being an invalid who is doomed to die.

But Frances Hodgson Burnett was a real gardener, who knew about sowing and planting and pruning, digging and weeding and thinning-out, and the Misselthwaite Manor garden is very much a real place, too, not just a pretty fancy. We can almost smell the newly turned earth and the sap of the grass roots, when Mary first digs with her wooden stick for hours, to free the newly shooting bulbs from the weeds which have been choking them for so long. There is nothing airy-fairy about the animals and plants and birds, flowers and grasses.

'Then Mary did a strange thing. She leaned forward and asked him a question she had never dreamed of asking anyone before. And she tried to ask it in Yorkshire because that was his language, and in India a native was always pleased if you knew his speech.

'"Does tha' like me?" she said'.

Within that short paragraph, some very deep and important things are said. Language meant a great deal to the author of *The Secret Garden*, and especially dialects and accents, people's own, personal way of speaking. By learning that language, understanding it and trying to speak it herself, Frances believed you got closer to people, and could share yourself with them. So, Mary tried to speak Dickon's Yorkshire, and so, later, does Colin.

When she was a girl, Frances got to know some of the poor factory children living nearby, and would hang about on corners, listening to their accents, encouraging them to talk to her, so that she could go away and try out the language herself in private. It helped her to feel a part of their strange lives, and put her in sympathetic touch with the kind of people they really were. So those people who speak and look and act differently in her books are never regarded as alien creatures, like visitors from other planets, but human beings who are surprising, and interesting partly because of those differences.

One quality essential to a writer of fiction is this kind of early interest in everything in life. Frances had it and later she attributed her success to it.

Anyone who has read the novels of the Brontë family will find in *The Secret Garden* some echoes of at least two of them: *Jane Eyre* by Charlotte, and *Wuthering Heights* by Emily Brontë. All writers are great readers and they are affected, deep within them, by particular books and other writers whose view of life strikes chords within themselves. Frances Hodgson Burnett does not borrow from, imitate or copy the Brontës' books; she is influenced by them in the best possible way; the echoes of them add some new layers of meaning to her own book, and in an odd way, to the Brontës' books, too. For all literature is linked together in one great dance, all writers share a deep imaginative relationship with one another.

Someone who wrote an essay about Frances Hodgson Burnett called *The Secret Garden* 'the most satisfying children's book I know'. And it is perfect to me. There are no false notes in it, everything fits – the place, the characters, the happenings, the dialogue, the atmosphere, the inner emotions, the descriptions, the whole shape of the story, all of these join together to make a work of art: satisfying, indeed. But it is more than 'a children's book', as all the best are, for it can be, and is, read and loved and reread by anyone, at any age.

Above all, and again, as with all the best books, when you have finished reading it, you will have been in some way affected and changed by it, deep within you, for always. And that is the real mark of a great book.

(1983)

Collected Ghost Stories

(Hamish Hamilton)

The traditional, classic English ghost story, like the traditional classic English detective story, has its origins in the nineteenth century. Of course, it is possible to trace elements that are essential to both much further back, to early mythological literature, and folk-lore. Nevertheless, as we recognise the forms, they were really Victorian; that period was when they were formed, that was when every self-respecting writer, good and bad, turned his or her hand to one, or both.

But, since the nineteenth century, the detective story has carried on its familiar way; although there have been various sub-divisions – the thriller, the spy-story – a great many of the detective novels that are still being published in such large numbers are cast in exactly the same mould as those written in the 1880s or the 1920s and '30s. Moreover, the detective story has gained, on the way, an intellectual snob-value – it is a form much dabbled in by dons. It is no shame – rather the contrary – to admit to being an addict, or a writer, of detective stories. But what about the ghost story? What about that once phenomenally popular form, without several examples of which no journal or magazine used to be complete? What happened to that?

Browse along the shelves of any public library which has a decent backstock, and you will find all manner of out-of-print collections, by individual, or assorted authors, most of them long-forgotten, of classic ghost stories. But browse in any bookshop and you will find, apart from the complete works of a very few masters of the form, like J. S. Le Fanu, nothing of the sort. You may be misled by paperbacks with lurid covers and titles that seem to be leading you in the right direction;

Tales of Horror, the Uncanny, the Supernatural, and Terror, will be their general style. Inside, you may possibly find one or two true ghost stories. But, on the whole, they will be something quite other, for the classic ghost story has gone a long way (and many would say downhill) in the direction of the gruesome, the crudely horrible, the weird, outlandish and fantastic. One of the first questions I was obliged to confront when I began to compile this anthology was, 'When is a ghost story not a ghost story?', and so far as anything written since the 1930s went I had to reply, 'Most of the time'.

So – what is *not* a ghost story? What did I rigorously exclude? Anything to do with werewolves, witches, vampires and monsters; anything science-fictional or about fantasy other-worlds inhabited by alien beings, however wraith-like their mere appearance might be; anything involving frightening occurrences which were bizarre, odd, inexplicable, in any ordinary, human terms, and yet which did not, apparently, involve 'ghosts' or, at least, ghostly phenomena. There is a masterly story of the macabre by Wilkie Collins, called *A Terribly Strange Bed*, in which a young man in nineteenth-century Paris visits a gambling house and is drugged and dragged upstairs by a crew of villains who have parted a good many other foolish young men from their money in this way; after robbing them, they murder them, as they almost murder the young narrator, by means of a bed which is built so that its canopy moves, by remote control, downwards, at the same time as its sides move inwards, to crush the sleeping victim to death beneath.

It is a sinister, heart-stopping tale, brilliant in its pacing, and its use of macabre detail. But it is not a ghost story. There is a practical, this-worldly explanation for every horrible happening.

The result of the rise of the tale of terror and horror was the decline in popularity of the classic ghost story. It was, at first, deemed not frightening enough. Worse, far worse, must happen, grim and dreadful and hair-raising incidents must be piled one on top of the other; blood must flow and be seen to flow, wounds must gape and stakes be driven through hearts. It was said that, as readers became more sophisticated and more informed about real, horrifying events in this world –

and, also, as they distanced themselves from superstitions and belief in a supernatural order – they became far less easily frightened, and so more and more grotesque and savage tales had to be fabricated before any flesh could be made to creep.

Virginia Woolf said as much, in her essay on 'Henry James's Ghost Stories' in 1921:

> The truth is perhaps that we have become fundamentally sceptical. Mrs Radcliffe amused our ancestors because they were our ancestors; because they lived with very few books, an occasional post, a newspaper superannuated before it reached them, in the depths of the country or in a town which resembled the more modest of our villages, with long hours to spend sitting over the fire drinking wine by the light of half a dozen candles. Nowadays we breakfast upon a richer feast of horror than served them for a twelvemonth. We are tired of violence; we suspect mystery.

And, a little further on in the same essay, she tells a writer of them that 'your ghosts will only make us laugh'.

In fact, laughter is precisely what is provoked by the horror film. As the incredible, grisly incidents are multiplied and become ever more fantastic and divorced from imaginable reality, the audience finds its release in mockery and gales of derisive laughter, rather than in shudders of fear.

Yet the classic ghost story still has tremendous power to chill and alarm, to make us turn our heads to look behind us and dread to walk up the dark staircase to bed at night. That is partly because its strength lies in under- not over-statement. Its art is the art of omission, of suggestion, not of crude and explicit description. But, even more important, it is frightening because it has its roots in the real world, the world we ourselves know and see and smell and touch and move about in, the world of houses, of furnished rooms, of tables and chairs, busy streets, of eating and drinking and conversation. And also because it strikes a chord with us of suspicion, of belief. We simply cannot, and do not, believe in werewolves and vampires, any more than we now believe in gorgons and dragons. But ghosts we can, and do – perhaps, indeed, *must* – believe in, however much we may say, in public, that we do not. Even if we do not believe in the external existence of a ghostly spirit of some person, now dead, who is appearing to us, in spectral shape, we believe in evil, and in forces within ourselves which can be externalised, actually or, at the very least, symbolically.

Investigations into psychic phenomena, including hauntings, became popular and widespread, with the ghost stories themselves, in the nineteenth century and they continue today, on a careful, scientific basis. Even if you discount ninety-nine per cent of them all, even if as many as that admit of some perfectly natural explanation, and even if one applies the principle of Occam's razor most rigorously, there is nevertheless that one per cent, that hard core of 'occurrences' which cannot be explained away. Ghosts exist. Certain places are haunted. Evil is sometimes made manifest and has power over certain individuals, circumstances, events.

But still, the ghost story, the tale of a quiet haunting, has declined in popularity, and, although it is certainly still written occasionally today, could scarcely be said to be thriving vigorously, as is the detective story.

One reason may be rather a mundane one. There have been a few outstanding examples of the ghost novel – *A Christmas Carol*, Henry James's *The Turn of the Screw* – but, on the whole, it is a short form, and very difficult to sustain over more than, say, ten thousand words or so. And short stories – individually or in collections – are simply not as popular as they were. Victorian readers devoured them by the dozen, in their variety of periodicals. But, since the last war, the number of magazines publishing them has gone on declining. And any novelist, however popular, who produces a collection of short stories, will notice a lower level of sales for these than for their full-length fiction.

Yet, because it can, in its quiet, simple way, arouse such an extraordinary response, the time would now seem to be ripe for a revival of the classic ghost story, in a world where an overkill of horror has begun to provoke a reaction of mere hilarity and boredom.

Charles Dickens was by no means the first nineteenth-century writer of ghost stories, but he was certainly its major populariser, responsible not only for writing a large number himself, but also for commissioning and publishing many others, in the magazines he edited. And the link between Dickens and the ghost story is strengthened by a further link between them both and the season of Christmas, which became the traditional time for the telling of ghost stories. The appearance of ghosts has long been associated, in legend and in religious mythology, with Christmas – though not, of course, exclusively so. The setting of the old house in the country, and the assembled company around a roaring fire, and the telling of a ghost story on Christmas Eve, became a classic one. M. R. James used to read aloud one of his own ghost stories to a group of friends, gathered together, in the light of a single candle; *The Turn of the Screw* opens in just such a setting.

It all works so well because what the ghost story writer must conjure up above all is atmosphere – his art relies almost exclusively upon it for its effect. The ghost story must impart a strong sense of place, of mood, of the season, of the elements, and so the traditional, haunted settings – old isolated houses, lonely churchyards, castles and convents and empty, narrow streets at night – are heavily relied upon. The worst writers of the Victorian ghost story, of course, simply piled on every spooky detail indiscriminately, in an effort to send shudders up the spine of the reader. The best writers are very carefully selective. For the history of the ghost story is precisely the history of an extraordinary mixture of the best and the worst of English fictional writing.

Before Dickens, there was Sir Walter Scott, whose fine ghost story 'Wandering Willie's Tale', in dialect, originally formed part of the novel *Redgauntlet*, and who wrote an essay on the supernatural in fiction which is one of the relatively few pieces of critical commentary on the form. Mrs Gaskell and Robert Louis Stevenson, Oscar Wilde and Henry James, Rudyard Kipling and H. G. Wells and Walter de la Mare, all wrote excellent ghost stories. More recently, Daphne du Maurier and Kingsley Amis have added beautifully to the repertoire, and Penelope Lively and Leon Garfield have made a corner all their own in the writing of ghost stories for children. But when I came to make my selection for this anthology it quickly became obvious that most of the entries would be from the period more than fifty and, in many cases, more than a hundred years ago.

In terms of literary quality, the stories chose themselves, though it was not easy, for example, to select finally between several equally good stories by Henry James or Kipling. But I made my definition of the classic ghost story very strict, and so a number of stories, excellent in themselves, did not fulfil all my conditions (including, for example, Thomas Hardy's 'The Withered Arm', and D. H. Lawrence's 'The Rocking Horse Winner', though both of them are brilliant stories of the supernatural).

Quite simply, I decided that a ghost story must have a ghost, and that the ghost must appear, or at least be heard, smelled or otherwise sensed. 'A ghost' was the spirit of some person, now dead, or else an embodiment of an evil force, or a strong emotion, such as distress or terror. It was not a demon, a dragon or Dracula.

On the other hand, the ghost might be seen as the projection of the (living) narrator's own psyche. (All Henry James's ghost stories fall into this category.) Nevertheless, they take external form and are described and seen as 'ghosts'.

I excluded stories in which the narrator or central figure saw his ghost while under the influence of drink, drugs or delirium; perhaps, in this, I was being a little over-scrupulous, but these do not seem to me to be true, ghostly apparitions, but hallucinations, which admit of real, medical or psychological explanations and do not 'exist' in any independent sense.

There are several writers known chiefly – or, indeed, only – as the authors of ghost stories: M. R. James, Arthur Machen, J. S. Le Fanu. Out of the works of the latter, who is perhaps the greatest ghost story writer of them all, it was particularly difficult to choose, but the two here are typical representatives of their genre, as well as being good in their own right. 'Green Tea' is a masterpiece, and 'The White Cat of Drumgunniol' can stand for a large number of stories about an apparition as a portent of death.

From that to Henry James's eminently civilised and even rather amusing and unfrightening ghost, 'Sir Edmund Orme', is a large step. A lot of writers worked more seriously in other forms, and treated their ghost stories as fun, but nothing

Henry James wrote was ever irrelevant to his consistently serious, artistic purpose – the investigation and understanding and complex portrayal of the human individual, in the context of his society. His ghost stories are serious, they are never pot-boilers, and neither are they ever written merely to make the reader's flesh creep. The effect they have is deeper and more permanent than that.

Rarely, at the other extreme, does a ghost story make one laugh. But Rhoda Broughton's curious tale of 'The Man with the Nose' is funny, to begin with at least, before the dreadful denouement, which foreshadows the much more chilling story of a ghostly abduction, Elizabeth Bowen's 'The Demon Lover'. And, until its final paragraphs, H. G. Wells makes us laugh, too, though increasingly hollowly and falteringly, at 'The Story of the Inexperienced Ghost'.

Kipling's story, 'They', moves one not to terror but to tears – indeed, it hovers on the edge of sentimentality but does not quite topple over and it is a particularly distinctive example of a common ghost story theme, a haunting by or of children. So is Mrs Gaskell's only excursion into the genre, 'The Old Nurse's Story', which is also rather moving.

There are several isolated houses here, but the most eerily unforgettable, the most atmospheric and unnerving, is surely Edith Wharton's Whitegates, cut off from the outside world by thick snow, on All Souls' Eve. Sense of place is also strong in M. R. James's classic, 'Oh, Whistle, and I'll Come to You, My Lad' – lonely shingle-shore and flat, open marshland will never seem the same to anyone who visits them, after reading it.

In a sense, every story is included here both for itself, and because it is a representative of many others. None of them is obscure, none has been dug out of long-lost Victorian periodicals, all are by well-known authors. What I wanted to assemble was simply a selection of the very best – best imagined, best written, best constructed – of a minor yet unjustly neglected English literary form. Ghost stories tell us a great deal about ghosts, and about living human beings, too, and about the relationship between them, and between the seen and the unseen worlds, the real and the supernatural, as well as between good and evil. They tell us about things that lie hidden within all of us, and which lurk outside all around us. They show human beings in the grip of the extremes of powerful emotions, at key moments and turning points in their lives. They also frighten delightfully, give shape, form and substance to our darkest and most primitive and child-like fears and imaginings, and, perhaps most importantly of all, they entertain and, like all good stories, hold 'children from play and old men from the chimney corner'.

(1983)

Corduroy

by Adrian Bell

(Oxford Paperbacks)

In any short list of the classic accounts of past life in the English countryside, which would include, for example, *Our Village* by Miss Mitford, Gilbert White's *A Natural History of Selborne*, and *Lark Rise to Candleford* by Flora Thompson among the best known and loved of titles, Adrian Bell's *Corduroy* would certainly take its place as the twentieth-century representative of that great tradition, had it not lain neglected and out of print for some years.

None of those authors set out to present for posterity a fully comprehensive picture of how men lived and worked, in riches or poverty, on farm and in the supportive trades and crafts, of how agriculture was planned, managed and practised and of the domestic system by which farmhouse and cottage were run, of British wildlife and flora, in meadow, woodland, hedgerow and ditch. Yet in aiming only at the small and particular, the local and immediate, they did accomplish that general view. Their books are highly personal, individual accounts, microcosms; they are observations of one village, one tiny area of a single county; they contain descriptions of men, women, and children in the manor house and the post office, the dairy farm and the rectory, the almshouse and in the overcrowded labourer's cottage. We overhear gossip and get to know people's idiosyncrasies of expression and habit; the birds seen on the roof of one barn on a December day in 1771 are recorded, as are the words written on the slate of one village schoolchild during a spelling lesson, the items sold to the vicar's housekeeper in the village store, and the length of time a farrier took to shoe the squire's chestnut mare. It is these transitory incidents, personal details seen and heard, that are set down, and so become representative of a whole way of life, a generation, an age; just as when John Constable painted a local farm boy whom he chanced to see lying on the ground beside his wagon, taking a drink of water from a stream, he gave us an image of much more general significance.

We do not only read the great chroniclers of English rural life in order to learn how things were; their books are far more than tracts of social history and geography. So too is *Corduroy*. Nevertheless, we *do* find out what life was like on a Suffolk farm in the first half of the twentieth century perhaps more accurately from Bell's rich, beautifully written volumes of autobiography (of which this is the first) than from many a text-book.

The succeeding parts, *Silver Ley* and *The Cherry Tree*, are well worth reading, as are the other country books Bell wrote, some of which were compiled from his weekly column, 'A Countryman's Notebook', which appeared for over thirty years in the *Eastern Daily Press*. They are informative and sensitive, the work of a highly individual thinker and of a natural stylist, of far more lasting value than mere journalism. But it is *Corduroy* alone which has that touch of genius, and a completeness, and poetic wholeness, which lifts it above so very many other good, sound books about English country life written in this century, and gives its author his proper place beside those earlier writers.

Corduroy is about the land of East Anglia and the life on it, about country people and animals, wild and domestic, about rural pursuits and the changing face of the land through the seasons. But it is principally about farming, and farming as it was before the Second World War and never will be again. The way of life it chronicles stretches back far into the past; in its essentials and in many details it has more in common with the times recorded by William Cobbett and Flora Thompson, Miss Mitford, and Francis Kilvert, than it has with the farming we know only a few decades later. Nothing has changed in itself or changed the landscape and the rural pattern and character of this country more than modern, mechanised, large-scale farming. The nature of the work from day to day and the attitudes and expectations of those engaged in it, the kind of crops grown, and how, the land on which it is all done, are so different today from those described in *Corduroy* that Bell's pages read like accounts of remote history. Even the animals are different, altered and standardised by selective breeding, streamlined housing, and artificial feeding; altered in character, behaviour, shape, and flavour. We read *Corduroy* and we discover how farming and farmers and the country they lived and worked in once were, and within living memory too, and if we wish, we can look upon the book as a lament, the still-life portrait of a vanished age.

But those are feelings that arise after reading the book, sad reflections based upon hindsight. While immersed in it, we are immersed in life, vigorous, practical, human, and natural, in all life's comedies and pantomimes, and in the everyday business of work on a farm. Most of all we are involved with the character of the young Adrian Bell, the green boy from London's Chelsea, who didn't know a horse's fetlock from a cow's udder when he persuaded his father to allow him a year, apprenticed to the long-suffering Mr Colville, in Suffolk, in which to discover if he took to and was cut out for, the farming life.

And it is this fact, that Bell was a learner and a looker-on, a newcomer to every aspect of the country and farming, which gives the book one of its particular distinctions; everything was fresh and strange to him, nothing was taken for granted, and so, in his account of that time, he misses nothing out as a result of long familiarity with it. We see, hear, feel everything as he did, all the impact things made upon him has been kept intact and comes directly at us through the vibrant prose. We smell the farmhouse kitchen at breakfast and the steaming stables on a frosty January morning. Bell makes us experience, just as he did, the terrifying lift and flight, the bone-jarring landing of an eager hunter leaping a five barred gate with a novice on his back, and the bone-ache in frozen, clumsy fingers as they struggle inexpertly with the heavy buckle and stiff thong of a harness, and the icy-cold metal of farm implements. *Corduroy* was written only ten years after Adrian Bell arrived, so wet behind the ears, at Mr Colville's mixed farm, on his motor-bike, and although those years brought him considerable experience and knowledge, as well as the ownership of a small farm, he still looks indulgently and never patronisingly back, upon his old, raw self; he laughs but he does not deride, exposes critically all the follies and errors which resulted from his total ignorance, but then he forgives, he does not reject, his youth. Still, when all that is said, the laughs at his own expense are very good ones, and he tells excellent stories against himself; about the brimming tankard of beer to which he was so unaccustomed, and how he surreptitiously poured it away, to the amused view of the publican's daughter who chanced to be looking from an upstairs window, and about the boots that he brought with him from London ('Those are gentleman's boots'), suited only to 'picnic lunches on green plateaux and those walks recommended in the week-end pages of the newspapers'; and about that first day out on the hunting field:

> Conversation was cut short for the moment because a piece of paper on the road woke up and flapped and the next I knew was that the horse and I were on the top of a steep bank and then on the road again twenty yards ahead. I found I was still on the horse's back. 'I shouldn't let her do that', said Mr Colville blandly.

And about the mistake over the farmhouse meal-time pattern, leading to over-indulgence in cheese and cocoa at bedtime, and to nightmares and dyspepsia thereafter.

As Adrian Bell describes his first, hard lessons in farm work, we gain, as he himself was gaining, a close insight into the exact nature of the country labourer's toil as it was over many centuries, how exhausting and demanding, how many individual skills were needed, and how long it took to master them, how serious for his own livelihood and the welfare of the animals in his care, not to mention his master's profits, a small mistake, a single, forgotten duty, could be. Simultaneously, we become aware of the responsibilities of the farmer himself, anxieties about weather and disease, predators and the swings of the market, concern for every man and creature in his charge. And through these insights we arrive at a deeper understanding not only of farmers and farm-workers and their occupations on the land, but of how others, especially writers, have seen and portrayed them wrongly; just as young Bell, after a hazardous morning learning the art of making a straight furrow with a horse-drawn plough, feels a kinship with the subject of one of Thomas Hardy's poems, 'Only a man harrowing clods', and a scorn of Hardy's own attitude to the man, 'despite the legend of his rural understanding'.

There are 'characters' in plenty enlivening the pages of the book; one of my favourites is old Stebling, who attributes his sixty years of robust health to the eating of nothing but pork and 'taters, with the occasional kipper taken raw 'bones and all', and who easily wins a shilling off the author by demonstrating his ability to lift a full pail of water by his teeth alone. People such as this are described vividly and succinctly, with affection and sometimes with amazement, but they are never caricatured or looked down upon; these are not the comic rustics of so many novels, but individuals, granted the dignity of their idiosyncrasies, never sentimentalised, nor unmanned by being presented as allegorical pastoral innocents – another common form of literary patronage.

Aside from the author himself, the hero of the book is Mr Colville, a man the like of whom could not be found in England today, and yet who is himself constantly regretting how times have changed for the worse and calling back the days of the old Squire! Mr Colville is shrewd, dictatorial, master of his little kingdom, occasionally contrary, but the successful manager of and respecter of his men, land, and animals, with a strong sense of family and tradition and locality, a robust taste for hunting and shooting, deep knowledge of the vagaries of weather and bank managers, and looking incongruously out of place dressed in shiny clothes in his wife's parlour on Sunday afternoon. He was the best tutor and example that a young apprentice farmer could have had. He is presented with all the skill of a practised novelist and, indeed, Adrian Bell had the novelist's touch altogether, the instinct for shaping and pacing his narrative, and varying its moods, the talent for sustaining a certain measure of suspense even over relatively mundane matters, and the ability to create an underlying stiffening of moral viewpoint. But as a young man in London he was an aspiring poet, and it is the poet's eye which lights upon the countryside, its changing moods and patterns, and selects and lovingly delineates some pertinent detail, and informs and infuses the whole text with a deep, subtle variety of feeling. There are some wonderful set-pieces gracing the book, written in lucid, natural prose, which sometimes rises to great heights, in that area where prose and poetry meet, though there is nothing at all lush or vague or indulgently fanciful about the style. Towards the end of *Corduroy* there is a passage describing how the harvest draws to a close, as, after another gloriously still, hot day, the huge moon rises over stacked sheaves and bare stubbled fields, all that was gold becomes silver, and the weary men and horses draw home the last loads, up through the lanes towards the barn. It is one of the most simply beautiful, elegiac pieces of descriptive writing about the English countryside that I know, plain and elegant, observed with accuracy and with love. It satisfies the heart.

So does the last page of the book, which closes one chapter and leads towards the opening of a fresh one, when Bell walks away, again at night, from Mr Colville's family party, and from his land and farmhouse, towards his own, the small farm his father has bought for him, where he will begin a new life, alone. It is at the same time poignant and vigorously forward-looking.

Appropriately enough, I first discovered *Corduroy*, and so the work of Adrian Bell, in a tiny second-hand bookshop in one of Suffolk's small villages so like that described in its pages. The copy that I bought then is an early paperback edition, now jacket-less and almost entirely broken apart through regular reading. That is the litmus test of this type of book; it must stand up to constant re-reading over many years, and give renewed delight each time, and there must be some aspect of it, some tiny detail of observation, a turn of phrase, a fact, an anecdote, that strikes one as though for the first time. All of which is true of *Corduroy*.

Its reappearance in print is long overdue and very welcome. Old friends will renew their acquaintance with it and, even more important, I hope it will win a wide new readership, for, as Q. D. Leavis wrote, shortly after Bell's death, 'his writings are literature, and should be kept in circulation as part of the English heritage'.

(1982)

The Third Miss Symons

by F. M. Mayor

(Virago Modern Classics)

It would be wrong to describe Flora Macdonald Mayor as a forgotten novelist, and inaccurate, too, at least to a certain extent, to claim that she is underrated. Her work is certainly far too little known in relation to the greatness of her talent. But her masterpiece, *The Rector's Daughter* (1924), is in print again (Penguin Modern Classics) and the ranks of its admirers are steadily increasing. Those who do discover her, pass the word along: biographical and critical studies of her are under way both here and in the United States, and this republication of *The Third Miss Symons* has been long awaited and can only help to increase her present-day reputation.

There is not, alas, much more of her fiction to be read, and what there is scarcely deserves resurrection. Her first novel, *Mrs Hammond's Children* (published under the pseudonym of Mary Strafford), is really interesting only by contrast with what came later. *The Squire's Daughter* (1929) is so poor that I find it hard to believe it was written by F. M. Mayor at all; a collection of mystery tales, in the sub-M. R. James tradition, *The Room Opposite* (published posthumously in 1935), are entertaining and certainly hold their own as minor representatives of a rather creaking genre.

But it is on the two novels alone that her claim to an important place in twentieth-century English fiction rests. They are works of a quite remarkable psychological depth, subtlety and assurance: they reveal a creative imagination and perceptiveness of devastating clarity and honesty, and demonstrate a technical mastery of the novel form which seems to be, as with all great writers, like a sixth sense, possessed and deployed with absolute confidence and ease.

The Third Miss Symons was published in 1913 and in style and tone belongs to its own day, and to the future, modern stream of English fiction. Nevertheless it looks backwards to the late Victorian era of social and feminine history, the final years of a settled, rigidly structured existence, before the Great War changed everything forever.

In the last resort, the novel has that air of timelessness possessed by all major works of art: it is artistically and humanly valid and relevant for always.

F. M. Mayor was born in 1872. She was enjoying her 30s, that first decade of true adulthood, when she wrote the novel. She, like her book, straddles the centuries. In some ways she was typical of a particular kind of educated Victorian/Edwardian spinster (with seven unmarried aunts!) yet she might also have been thought of, in her own day, as a representative of the new, emancipated woman.

Her father, a clergyman, was Emeritus Professor of Classics at King's College, London, and author of many books. Her mother was a niece of the historian George Grote. Her paternal uncle, also a parson, was Professor of Latin at Cambridge. It was to Cambridge that Flora went, to read history at Newnham, an unusual, though not by then a pioneering thing for a young woman to do at the turn of the century. A far more remarkable fact is that she went on the professional stage, with the Ben Greet company, for a time after graduating. As her niece, Lady Rothschild, writes, 'Imagine at that date a clergyman's daughter from such an intransigently high-minded, classical background, doing such a thing'.

Certainly it would have provided her with experience of a world far removed from that in which she had so far lived and, more important, a novel perspective on that world, and particularly on the place of the women in it. Miss Mayor was intelligent, independent and enterprising, and to some degree placed herself for a time outside her own background and social position, but she was not a rebel, and when she began to write, it was about that society she had always known, the women of the provincial middle-classes in the years around the turn of the century. Henrietta 'the third daughter and fifth child of Mr and Mrs Symons' is typical, at least in circumstances, of thousands of women of her generation and class, and the complete opposite of her creator, for she has no independence of spirit, not a trace of enterprise or individual courage. She neither seeks out opportunities nor seizes those few which come her way.

John Masefield, in his Introduction to the first edition of the novel, described how 'her brain like so many of the brains in civilisation is but slightly drawn upon or exercised: she is not so much wasted as not used. Having by fortune and tradition nothing to do, she remains passive till events and time make her incapable of doing. She has done nothing but live, and been nothing but alive'.

F. M. Mayor was writing about a previous generation: by her own day a few more doors had opened, at least to a young woman of her determined character. It is difficult to imagine both the claustrophobia and the enervating oppressiveness of the tedious lives Henrietta and her kind were obliged to pursue and, even more, to sympathise with a woman so depressed, so lacking in energy and spirit as to submit to its restrictions without a struggle, and with only the sort of protest that turns inward, and festers, to manifest itself merely in the form of pettiness and ill-temper.

The fault lies in Henrietta's personality as much as in her circumstances. She knows it, at least in her heart of hearts, and loathes herself, and can do nothing to escape from the prison of herself.

It is hard indeed to like her or sympathise with her, or to enjoy her company, hard not to want to give her a good shake. Yet her creator manages to write 140 pages in which there is precious little relief from her, to catalogue all her faults, to convey the impatience of her relatives and acquaintances (for she can scarcely be said to have friends) with her – and yet to view her compassionately, to awaken our understanding and sympathy, to make allowances and, finally, to redeem.

It is a profoundly sad, profoundly moving book; its ending might so easily have seemed sentimental, bathetic, or at least quite unconvincing. It is none of those things. It works, it is credible, it stirs one to tears. F. M. Mayor was a Christian, not merely because she had an upbringing in a conventionally clerical household, but because she believed in the essential tenets of the Christian faith – in love, in basic human affinity, and brotherhood, in salvation, forgiveness and compassion, and in redemption and resurrection.

We are irritated and bored by Henrietta; after her death her sister Evelyn blames herself for being neglectful and loving her too little. She says, 'It was all my fault'. But F. M. Mayor knows that it is the novelist's great power, and responsibility, to discern and tell the truth. And the truth is that it was not Evelyn's fault 'but Henrietta's own: that it was because she was so unlovable that she was so little loved'.

Yet a still greater truth follows, at a deeper level. 'If she had had the chance she wouldn't have been unlovable'.

The novel is the story of Henrietta's personality; its shape, the shape of her life, is a vicious circle. She becomes less and less lovable because, from the beginning of her life, she is hardly loved. Children know rejection when they meet it, and quickly assume that they are not loved because they are not worthy of love. From the opening sentence, Miss Mayor strikes a chill note; the dice are loaded against Henrietta, because of her very position in the family – 'enthusiasm for babies had declined in both parents by the time she arrived'.

The battle for affection and attention was over as soon as it had begun. Henrietta does have her hour. 'At five, her life attained its zenith. She became a very pretty, charming little girl'. But the flowering is brief enough. At eight 'her charm departed never to return and she slipped back into insignificance'.

What Henrietta fails to do, throughout her life, is seize the fleeting opportunity, consolidate her position and then improve upon it, whether by behaving attractively or learning to be ingratiating. The moment things start to go wrong for her, she becomes sour and resentful, and allows her ill-temper free rein.

And sometimes the very force of her own longing for love causes her to act desperately and so lose it.

Things improve with the birth of her younger sister Evelyn and it is this relationship which is at the heart of Henrietta's life until the end, unsatisfactory in many ways though it is – for her own rudeness, tactlessness and short-temper put it under severe strain. Its culmination is unbearably poignant. At one stage, for one night, the sisters draw closer than they have been since childhood, meeting each other face to face, sharing confidences, speaking truths. Afterwards Evelyn scarcely remembers it, absorbed by husband and children. To Henrietta it has been all in all. After her death, Evelyn finds a note hidden in a box. It says 'I can't tell you how much good you have done me, I seem to have been living for this for fifteen years. Evelyn, September 23, 1890.'"

A whole life, and so little salvaged, such a morsel of affection cherished through years of loneliness, purposelessness, unhappiness.

Clearly, one of Henrietta's chief enemies is boredom, and although it is certain that other, more enterprising and robust, or else sweetly acquiescent, uncritical natures did survive the tedium and narrowness of such lives, nevertheless it was more difficult for a woman, especially a spinster, to break out.

'Even now when there is a certain amount of choice and liberty, a woman who is thrown on her own resources at thirty-nine with no previous training and no obvious claims and duties does not find it very easy to know how to dispose of herself. But a generation ago, the problem was far more difficult'.

Once Henrietta's single chance of securing a husband (if a real chance it is) has been lost, she resigns herself to spinsterhood. Her sisters quickly marry, after which there are no more parties. Henrietta lingers at home, a low-spirited companion for her ailing parents, dabbling in the idea of reading Italian. After her mother's death, she housekeeps for father and brothers but she is domineering, ill-tempered, inefficient. Her father remarries, Henrietta is displaced, and the household runs smoothly and happily again, so that she realises that 'she had had her chance, her one great chance in life, and she had missed it'. After that she lives mostly abroad, wandering pointlessly from one shabby-genteel pension to another, occasionally sight-seeing without any pleasure, otherwise playing patience because during a game 'the clock had moved from ten minutes past eight to twenty five minutes to ten'.

Her remaining years are spent in Bath, and although her daily occupations – tea parties, church affairs, the drinking of the spa waters – seem petty beyond belief, somehow she is busier and happier, and though she does not find love, she makes acquaintances, and has a loyal maid.

The days of her dying are marvellously described. Evelyn is abroad and does not receive the vital telegram which arrives too late. She discovers her sister's pathetic souvenirs, along with the note, in a little box, experiences remorse and then, suddenly, unaccountably, a mystical revelation, which is so convincing, and which redeems and transforms everything that has gone before, the whole novel, the whole of Henrietta's life, without in any way overriding or minimising the actual 'bitterness, aimlessness and emptiness' of it whilst it was being lived.

The book is an extraordinary many-faceted study of one woman, presented to us both from the eyes of its creator, and those outside of her, and at the same time from within – a complex achievement. F. M. Mayor has a devastating ability to make clear statements, generalisations that stem from innumerable minutely particular observations about human life, behaviour and society, so that we gasp at the simple enormity of what she is saying and see at once that it is the plain truth.

She is sensitive yet detached, firm and decisive in her prose style, infinitely various and subtle in her method of approach, and each reading of *The Third Miss Symons* yields up more riches. How very little material she is handling after all – and yet she is holding the whole of human life in her hand and subjecting it to scrutiny, recreating it for us. She evinces deep sympathy and understanding. I cannot believe that anyone could read the novel without coming away from it changed, illuminated, made wiser and more understanding of its heroine and her life and times, and of the human condition in general.

(1983)

The Distracted Preacher and Other Tales

by Thomas Hardy

(Penguin Classics)

It was to poetry that Thomas Hardy finally and completely committed himself as a creative artist; it is as a novelist that he is best and most widely known and celebrated – he is at least as popular today among ordinary readers as during his own lifetime. Both Hardy the poet and Hardy the novelist have received a great deal of scholarly attention and acclaim, and, in addition, the life and personality of Hardy the man have aroused fascinated interest.

By contrast, his short stories have fared poorly, receiving relatively scant and dismissive treatment at the hands of many commentators, and being nowadays too little read, partly as a result of this critical neglect, partly because the short story itself has rather fallen out of favour. Yet they form a significant and decent-sized portion of his work – there are forty-nine stories in all, four full volumes in the Wessex edition, out of which I have chosen eleven (arranged in chronological order of first publication) which are among the best and the most representative; the most grudging assessment should allow that well over half of the total are very good as stories, and of considerable interest for the reflective light they throw on the rest of Hardy's prose fiction. Some are masterpieces, and even the failures partake of his total imaginative vision, and fail in such a characteristically Hardyan way that they make a contribution to our understanding of his art and technique.

Above all, though, they are eminently readable and delightfully accessible; they do not intimidate. Those aspects of Hardy's writing which most often irritate or repel – the syntactical mannerisms and convolutions, the archaisms and insensitively placed abstract or learned references – are largely absent from the stories.

The prose style is direct and lucid, relaxed, yet simultaneously maintaining a tension which both holds the reader and carries the narrative forward, and which allows for as much revelation as the form itself will hold, and some development of character. There is descriptive writing, scene-painting of an evocative and occasionally breathtaking kind (as in the picture of the army camp on the Downs at early morning, in *The Melancholy Hussar*). Telling details are selected and set in like jewels, but because he had not the space in which to spread and indulge himself, Hardy responds by making a virtue of economy, restraint and simplicity.

Because the stories were not produced out of a spontaneous bubbling-up of inspiration to which he could not choose but attend, but always in response to a direct request from the editors of magazines and for money, they have been branded as pot-boilers in more than the most obvious sense and seen as suffering from all the worst effects of hasty conception and cursory production. In some cases this is true. But much that is best, straightforward and simple about the stories and, more important still, most suitable to the form itself, seems to me to arise just because Hardy did not worry anxiously over them. The more seriously he took his fiction the more he was inclined to fret, and this fretting affected his style. The worst obscurities and complexities which sometimes tangle the surface of his prose are not so much a result of his grappling with complex intellectual, philosophical and moral issues, and failing to express them in fictional terms – though he often was so grappling and sometimes he failed – as of a touching but misguided desire to impress, to appear sophisticated in learning.

But in his short stories he is dedicated simply to the business of telling a tale well and being done; and though there are historical and classical allusions and a sprinkling of recondite words and phrases – and these are by no means always merely redundant decorations – there are few stylistic obstructions to the reader's immersion in, and thorough appreciation of, the narrative.

Nevertheless, it would be doing Hardy a disservice if an

attempt to right the balance and to win a wider and more admiring public for his short stories spilled over into an uncritical and blanket enthusiasm. I have said that some of them are failures; others are seriously limited or flawed and, paradoxically, just as his more relaxed and brisk approach to the writing of stories tended to bring out some of the best and keep at bay some of the worst aspects of his art, so it gave rise to the greatest faults, of attitude and of construction.

Coincidence often reaches out a long arm in Hardy's fiction. Lives are altered in their courses, fates are determined and plots resolved by chance, bad luck or, as some see it, the machinations of a malevolent fate. So it is in life, and the extent to which Hardy loads the dice has been exaggerated. It is the prerogative, even the purpose, of the artist to emphasise and underline particular aspects of the raw material which he takes from nature; this is one of the means by which he transforms that material and imbues it with his own creative vision and personality, before shaping it into his own pattern. As Hardy himself put it: 'Art is a changing of the actual proportions and order of things, so as to bring out more forcibly . . . that feature in them which appeals most strongly to the idiosyncrasy of the artist'.[1]

In his best novels and stories he does this and still maintains a balance. Some of the events, both life-shaping and incidental, come about because certain characters behave in certain ways – what they do, or refrain from doing, or cause to happen to them, is a direct result of the kind of people they are; other events are imposed on them from without, by chance – or the author himself – and we are asked to accept, to suspend disbelief in and be convinced by, the whole work of fiction and its outcome. It may be more difficult to achieve this balance in the short story, which has a number of inbuilt pitfalls, but it is perfectly possible, as Hardy demonstrates in some of the best of them.

But he can also be cursory in the extreme, imposing a plot like a heavy corset which stifles any potential life underneath. A deadline, insufficient commitment to, and thought about, a particular story, low imaginative intensity and lack of sus-

1. *The Life of Thomas Hardy* by Florence Emily Hardy.

tained care, all of these contribute to the cavalier attitude which can produce wooden, two-dimensional characters, manipulated by the author and at the mercy of chance events, being pushed towards the thud of an artificial conclusion.

There may be little excuse for this and Hardy must have been aware that, to say the least, he was not giving of his best on these occasions. But to do him justice, it is possible that his creative mind was elsewhere, for he was producing most of the short stories over the same period of years as many major novels, including *The Mayor of Casterbridge*, *The Woodlanders*, *Tess of the d'Urbervilles* and *Jude the Obscure*.

Because they have not always seemed satisfactory as examples of the short story, various efforts have been made to reclassify them, as 'ballads' or 'tales'. Certainly there are some typical elements of the ballad in them – the frequent use of a narrator and discursive unfolding of dramatic, even bizarre events in a homely setting; and Hardy himself chose the title *Wessex Tales* for the first published collection, though any distinctions made between 'tale' and 'story' are unconvincing beyond a certain elementary point. But the change of nomenclature can be helpful if it serves as a reminder of the period at which they were written – the late nineteenth century – and the fact that that was well before the development of the modern short story as we know it in the work of Katharine Mansfield, say, or D. H. Lawrence and Hemingway, or (though he was in fact Hardy's contemporary) Henry James. Otherwise we shall expect of Hardy what he was not intending or equipped to give.

He has suffered considerably from the myths which have arisen as a result of repeated exaggerations and distortions of his text, and one of the commonest fallacies is that he was quintessentially a country-man who wrote almost exclusively of country matters and, moreover, that the country characters who feature predominantly in his books are the unlettered, unskilled, agricultural working class. He wrote of them, of course, but only occasionally, just as he was concerned for only part of the time with events in a remotely rural setting. Hardy was a man of social and intellectual aspirations and achievements, who worked and lived in London and continued to spend five months of every year there after he had made his permanent home in Dorset. Many of his short stories are set in the *towns* of Wessex and are about the professional middle classes, teachers, lawyers, clergy, businessmen, and their families. Often they concern the rise of such people, like Hardy himself, from humbler and more deeply rural origins, their ambitions for education, wealth and social status and the tensions to which such ambitions give rise, between past and present, old and new friends and loyalties, beliefs and values, habits and manners.

Even in the more exclusively country tales, unskilled labourers are in the minority, and the background; the characters are farmers, often comfortably set-up, landowners and employers, or else the tradespeople, shopkeepers and craftsmen of the market towns.

One complete group is separate from the rest: the county aristocracy. Hardy writes of the skeletons in their cupboards – illegitimacy, murder, insanity, incest – in the rather unsuccessful collection, *A Group of Noble Dames*. These people are neither rising nor falling, but have long been firmly settled at the top of the ladder, and Hardy also sets them, for the most part, in the eighteenth century, so that the whole effect is of distance and isolation from the general stream of life and their static situation leads to a deadness in the stories.

The fact that Hardy is very good indeed at portraying women, that he understood them intuitively and reveals most convincingly their inner natures and psychological subtleties as well as their outward appearance and behaviour, has been so emphasised that his male characters are sometimes seen, by contrast, as weak and two-dimensional, existing in the shadow of the women in whom the writer was really interested.

If we look at some of his fiction, we may see how the impression arose. If we look at the whole of it, the balance is at once restored. The short stories contribute to that balance, for they are dominated here by women, here by men, of a variety of kinds, though with certain psychological types recurring. A number of the women – Ella Marchmill in *An Imaginative Woman*, Lizzy in *The Distracted Preacher*, Edith Harnham in *On the Western Circuit* – are restless, lively and bored, educated and intelligent enough to yearn to break out of the confines of limited rural society and its repetitious activities, or prosaic, claustrophobic marriage. It is a familiar figure in Hardy and typically, it is a personality which provokes behaviour leading to misfortune and disaster. There are also single country girls who suffer at the hands of the clever and sophisticated, often a townee and usually male, and when he is concerned with men, Hardy frequently examines their ambitions or insensitivity or hypocrisy in a full and steady light. But he can portray the plain, good man beautifully – Ned Hipcroft in *The Fiddler of the Reels* – as well as the rogue, the solid citizen, the eccentric, the bully and the fool.

But whether the focus of the author's attention is a man or a woman in any particular story, the relationship between them is the theme of almost all. Hardy was preoccupied with affairs of the heart, with love requited or frustrated, fulfilled or doomed, with the meetings, partings, deceptions and self-deceptions of lovers – the whole business of courtship and romance, and the disillusion and distress, or mere tedium, of any subsequent matrimony. A few of the couples are ordinary enough but in the short stories, as in the novels, we are brought up time and again against an even more specific and idiosyncratic aspect of sexual affairs. John Bayley puts it succinctly: 'Hardy's favourite theme is an incongruous love situation in a peculiar setting'.[1]

Such a theme features in all but one (*The Grave by the Handpost*) of the stories collected here, and in a good proportion of the rest. Hardy worried at it throughout his fiction-writing career, setting up couple after oddly-assorted couple, studying the perverseness of human nature in romantic and sexual matters from various angles and pursuing its outcome to many bitter conclusions. There are discrepancies of social class between the lovers (*The Son's Veto*), age (*A Mere Interlude*), temperament and character (*The Distracted Preacher*), intelligence and education (*On the Western Circuit*) and nationality (*The Melancholy Hussar*).

But it is noteworthy that although individual scenes may provide an element of the 'peculiar setting', in general the backgrounds are rather less extraordinary than in several of the

1. *An Essay on Hardy* (Cambridge University Press, 1978).

novels. Hardy's fascination with the unusual, the bizarre, grotesque and macabre, is certainly in evidence in these stories: Baptista Trewthen lies in bed in a hotel room, between the living body of her present husband and the dead one of his predecessor (*A Mere Interlude*); Gertrude Lodge visits the county gaol after a public execution in order to touch the corpse of the hanged man with her withered arm; Barbara of the House of Grebe is horrified out of her love for her former husband by being obliged by her sadistic new one to contemplate his mutilated statue.

This aspect of the writer and its place in his work as a whole can also be over-stressed. It is not only that Hardy was by no means unusual or obsessive among imaginative writers, and, indeed, other artists, in his taste for the odd and the gruesome, particularly when set in juxtaposition with more mundane matters – rather the contrary. Much more importantly, a realisation both of his inclination towards the weird, and of the carefully controlled and very limited part it actually plays in his fiction, serves to underline his self-control and artistic sensitivity and restraint. His skill in inserting a grotesque or morbid incident or detail at exactly the right point, so as to achieve maximum effect, is immense. It is on the few occasions when he piles up horrors or peculiarities gratuitously that he is an unsatisfactory, because unbalanced, writer. For, on the whole, Thomas Hardy is an infinitely more balanced artist than he has been made to appear.

However, it is not the occasional bizarre touches which alienate some readers but what is felt to be the improbability of his stories in general, particularly those with the most strikingly unusual characters and eventful plots. Certainly Hardy did not believe that it was the job of a fiction-writer simply to serve up a slice of mundane, everyday life, but the extravagance of his plots is often more apparent than real, and for the most part the action lies well within the bounds of both psychological and practical credibility. In a note of 1893 he makes it penetratingly clear that he was acutely conscious of the essential and delicate nature of these problems:

> A story must be exceptional enough to justify its telling. We tale-tellers are all Ancient Mariners, and none of us is

> warranted in stopping Wedding Guests (in other words, the hurrying public) unless he has something more unusual to relate than the ordinary experience of every average man and woman.
>
> The whole secret of fiction and the drama – in the constructional part – lies in the adjustment of things unusual to things eternal and universal. The writer who knows exactly how exceptional and how non-exceptional his events should be made, possesses the key to the art.[1]

That quotation, and especially the second paragraph of it, seems to me to sum up the aims and achievements of Hardy's fiction and to indicate the very reason for its existence. And once again it is when, for whatever reason, he fails to get the balance right between what he calls 'things unusual' and 'things eternal and universal', the exceptional and the ordinary, that it is hard to suspend disbelief in the result.

Nevertheless, we should not go to Hardy at all if we do not want to be told a rare tale, to be amazed, disturbed and intrigued, and it is his insistence upon the necessity of a writer having something extraordinary to relate that reveals how firmly rooted he is in a past tradition – the tradition of, among others, the balladist, the storyteller sitting with a group of listeners around a fire.

When this aspect of him is to the fore, and when the stories are thoroughly country stories, often containing some of the traditional, oral superstitions and folk-lore of the Wessex people, Hardy is unmistakably a writer belonging to his own or an earlier century.

The explanation of his ability to arrest and retain the reader's attention lies partly in the nature of the stories he chooses to tell, but just as much in his way of telling them, the sheer narrative skill. That is not an easy quality to analyse; it depends upon an innate sense of length and pace, which in turn are related to prose style and its rhythms, and the careful proportions of and balance between description, dialogue and the straightforward recounting of events and actions, together

1. *The Life of Thomas Hardy* by Florence Emily Hardy.

with a knowledge of exactly what to put in and what to leave out, what to state and what to imply.

The opening of a story serves one of the most crucial functions of all. Upon its power and effectiveness, the hold over the reader's attention and the success of the complete narrative structure depend.

The novelist may begin in any one of a number of possible ways, approach his story from a variety of different angles and – even though some will be more suitable than others – still achieve essentially the same result, produce the same novel in the end, no matter which he chooses. It is not simply that he has more time and space because the novel is longer, but that the novel is an essentially different literary form from the short story; it has more dimensions and can successfully contain more irregularities and discrepancies within itself. A good novel can survive and overcome a weak, diffuse or misdirected opening; a short story almost never can.

With very few exceptions the openings of Hardy's short stories are masterly and absolutely suited to the rest of what follows. His most typical way of beginning (and it is true of the novels also) is to set a scene, and if we examine carefully how he does so we understand at once one of the reasons why his books and stories have been so successful when adapted to the cinema or television screen, for he uses, as it were, the camera's eye, first standing well back and sweeping broadly over an extensive landscape, before zooming in to pick out and scrutinise a smaller detail – one cottage, or hut, a solitary traveller on the road that traverses a barrow. The method is the same when he moves from a general view of a street or a group of people, to fix his attention on one house, one individual.

Some abstract conclusions have been drawn from the way Hardy often sets the small figures of men and women and creatures against a vast landscape; it has been seen as the overriding image of a whole philosophy about the insignificance and minuteness of human beings and the huge aloofness and impersonality of nature. Such an implication is certainly contained in these scenes and our general impression of their meaning is a valid one, but it is a mistake to see Hardy's intentions as always or exclusively metaphorical. He is often simply a watcher, a depicter and describer, with the eye of a camera or of a landscape painter; he is selecting and giving artistic emphasis to and putting a frame around what he sees, to create a remarkable and arresting visual image which will lead us into a fascinating human story. In a part of the country where the downs are high and exposed to the elements and the sky, and there are few trees to break the continuous eyeline for miles, a human being, on foot or on horseback, or a single dwelling, does inevitably appear tiny and dominated by nature.

When he is beginning a novel, Hardy expands his passage of descriptive scene-setting, wandering in at a discursive pace towards the point at which characters about whom the plot is to centre are observed, then introduced. He cannot use this relaxed method of opening a short story, yet very little seems to be lost, so good is he at painting his scene in a few swift, economical strokes, being sparing yet also exact and telling in his use of detail, and leaving a satisfying amount to the imagination of the individual reader.

Of the other principal types of opening used by Hardy, one, in which a narrator takes the pipe out of his mouth or sets down his glass, clears his throat and introduces the tale, belongs firmly to the old-fashioned, ballad-style tradition; the other seems to bring Hardy forward in time to take his place in style and spirit among twentieth-century short story writers. The method is direct, even abrupt. Instead of being led slowly, and from a distance, towards setting and characters, we are put straight down in their midst at a point when events are already under way.

> When William Marchmill had finished his inquiries for lodgings at the well-known watering place of Solentsea in Upper Wessex, he returned to the hotel to find his wife.
>
> (*An Imaginative Woman*)

Instead of the focus narrowing gradually from a wide general view down to smaller and more particular details, it fixes straight away on such a one.

> To the eyes of a man viewing it from behind, the nut-brown hair was a wonder and a mystery. Under the black

beaver hat surmounted by its tuft of black feathers, the long locks, braided and twisted and coiled like the rushes of a basket, composed a rare, if somewhat barbaric, example of ingenious art.

(*The Son's Veto*)

In both these instances, and in others, the style of opening seems to suit the setting – in town, not country – and the more educated and sophisticated personalities of the protagonists.

I have said that most of Hardy's short stories, and all of his novels, are principally about love affairs. They have another common element – a character, of whatever kind, who plays a particular role upon which the story pivots. The role is that of the intruder, the person coming, in one sense or another, from outside the secure circle which is at the heart of the story, to disrupt and disturb, threatening and breaking up the established order of things, and it is often inextricably bound up with the love relationship – the very thing, indeed, that makes it an incongruous one. In *The Distracted Preacher* the intruder is Stockdale, the minister, arriving among the closely-knit villagers, all of whom are involved in the smuggling, and in any case an outsider and destined to remain so by the very fact of his being a clergyman. Just as Matthäus Tina is automatically one because he is a foreigner, though in *The Melancholy Hussar* it is the whole regiment who are intruders into the quiet, circumscribed life of the neighbourhood. In *On the Western Circuit* the lawyer Raye breezes in from London and from the professional classes, into the small-town lives of Edith Harnham and the simple maid, Anna, to cause emotional (and in Anna's case, physical) disruption. Seduction is sometimes the form the intrusion takes. Wat Ollamoor, the demonic fiddler of the reels invades the village and the hearts and bodies of its girls, causing moral breakdown and widespread misery.

But the stranger from without is not necessarily male. Gertrude, in *The Withered Arm*, coming to this part of the country for the first time as Lodge's bride, is the outsider, ignorant of the situation that formerly existed between her husband and Rhoda Brook and of the present *status quo*, as well as of local superstitions and customs. And in *An Imaginative*

Woman the stranger, the poet Robert Trewe who invades Ella Marchmill's heart and provokes the hysterical behaviour which leads to marital tragedy, is not even aware of his role.

The device is useful because it establishes a clear and satisfying narrative pattern, and yet it is at the same time capable of endless permutations and enables incident to be dependent upon and emerge from the characters and their relationships. Hardy's use of the intruder figure is regular and interesting, but it would be misleading to draw too many conclusions about his artistic psychology from its prominence in his work, for it is one of the basic themes of literature and forms an element in ballads, tales and short stories, both well before and after Hardy's time. In this, as in so many other aspects of his fiction, he is rooted firmly in the past English tradition.

Yet however true this may be, the real reason we read and admire Hardy is because he is *Hardy*, with a literary persona, a creative intelligence and an imaginative vision uniquely and unmistakably his own; and, when all questions of prose style, subject matter, location, character-type and personal philosophy have been taken into account, he possesses that extra quality which is, in the last resort, indefinable, as such things always are. The short stories add to, enrich and expand our knowledge and appreciation of him because they are so clearly and inseparably part of his work, and because they are permeated by that atmosphere, narrative power and vivid and deep sense of place and its intimate relation to character which are the essentials of Hardy's genius.

(1979)

I'm the King of the Castle

by Susan Hill

(Longmans Imprint Edition)

Almost all imaginative writers (novelists, poets, playwrights) have obsessions – subjects, themes, images, character-types, settings, which recur over and over again in their work, perhaps for many years. They are fascinated by them, pick them up and turn them over and over, to examine them from different angles, worry at them, as dogs worry bones. Sometimes, they do write the obsessions out of themselves and that's that; forever afterwards, their interest in the subject is dead.

These obsessions, these favourite themes, don't reappear in exactly the same guise, they are developed, altered, gone into more deeply. If they were simply repetitions, both writer and reader would very soon get bored and abandon the piece of work.

Obsessions are a bit like a writer's style, they are signature tunes, recognisable, idiosyncratic, personal; or like handwriting, perhaps, and they tell us just as much about that particular writer and the nature of his inner world, his creative imagination, and how it works.

Where they come from, how they become obsessions at all, is hard to fathom but clues can usually be found way back in the writer's past, and especially in his childhood, that rich fossil-ground and treasure house, held forever somewhere within him, the strongest lifetime influence upon him and his work. The first fourteen years or so of a writer's life are by far the most important, though of course, everything he ever sees, hears, feels, senses, learns, reads, may become grist to his fictional mill. (Or it may not, and he can never decide that for himself, except in the most superficial sense, the process of sorting out what will eventually be memorable and important enough to find a place, however small, in his work, goes on the whole time, deep in the subconscious.)

One of my own strongest and regularly recurring obsessions has been with childhood; my own, indirectly, but more, the state of childhood; what it feels like, how it truly is and how adults misinterpret it. And particularly, I have been interested in children who are in some way at odds with the rest of the world. (This is by no means an unusual obsession for a novelist; it was a principal theme for Charles Dickens, for example, and coming into our own day, Elizabeth Bowen and William Trevor have returned to it again and again.) I have also been obsessed by characters who are still stuck in this unhappy, misfit state, for all manner of reasons, when they reach adult years – it's an extension of and a variation upon, the same obsession. Both Mrs Kingshaw and Mr Hooper, in *I'm the King of the Castle*, are to some extent still at odds with the normal, adult world.

But it is the boys on whom I concentrate. Kingshaw and Hooper are both – well, *what* are they? It's hard to find exactly the right word, so misfits will have to serve. They are what very, very many people feel themselves to be, at some time or another. Neither of them relates, in a normal, easy, open way, a way that comes naturally as breathing to others, and especially to adults. Hooper dislikes his father, and feels removed from him; he is a cold boy, calculating, self-centred, manipulative, both a bully and a coward. His way of relating to other people is to try to have power over them, or to judge them – he can only cope in a world which is organised as he chooses, to suit himself. Of course, it is perfectly normal to feel at odds with one's parents, and isolated from them, but both Kingshaw and Hooper are like this all the time, and in an extreme way – not so normal.

Charles Kingshaw is the sort of boy who some would call 'sensitive', and others would call 'neurotic' – it all depends on your point of view. Really, he is both. He has been able to relate, to a limited extent, at his first school, by disappearing, being anonymous, the boy whose name nobody ever remembers, and who looks rather like any number of other boys.

That is his way of coping with an extreme fear of life, until he comes to Warings and encounters Edmund Hooper, the malevolent bully. Then fear consumes him, and he cannot sink back into the comfort of the crowd; he is a coward. Re-reading the book, I was struck by the extent and number of his fears; almost anything, real or imaginary, frightens him, and there is no doubt that, although many of these fears are understandable, even though irrational, some of the time one does want to shake him, tell him to pull himself together, stop being such a weed, face his terrors, stand his ground . . . all those bracing clichés that are commonly used apply here, and the sense behind them is in some measure right. If *only* he had the nerve to call Hooper's bluff once or twice, if only he could build upon his experience of Hooper's own cowardice, when they are lost in the wood. But he cannot, he does not, and that is his undoing.

Kingshaw is dominated by terror, and fear is the most appalling emotion to have to live with, day in day out, it is draining, depressing and demoralising. The future, once Kingshaw is told he is to go off to boarding school with Hooper, seems to hold out no hope at all; the fears will remain, the torments will be more varied and numerous, the prospect before Kingshaw's imagination is terrible indeed.

I have often been taken to task for the ending of the novel. It couldn't, wouldn't happen, it is melodramatic and unlikely, it *shouldn't* happen. No boy of eleven would commit suicide because he's afraid of a bully.

But boys of eleven *have* committed suicide for what, to the adult outsider, might seem even flimsier reasons. Children and young people *do* occasionally kill themselves. I knew a girl of fourteen who killed herself because her father was going to remarry a woman she could not bear the idea of as her stepmother (though she seemed nice enough to everyone else). In Japan, children have committed suicide because they are overworked at school, and under too much pressure there, and at home, to pass examinations, do well, do better than anyone else, 'get on'. Time, when you are eleven, still moves relatively slowly, and the future for Kingshaw, six or seven years of Hooper at home and at school, is an eternity ahead. I believed in his suicide when I made it happen, and, re-reading the book, I believe in it all over again.

Kingshaw and his mother had some forerunners, in the novel I wrote before this one, called *A Change for the Better*. There, a self-possessed, thoughtful, intelligent boy, James Fount, lives with his mother, a woman, like Mrs Kingshaw, who is disappointed, rather silly, a little genteel, fading into middle-age. They do not understand each other at all. So, the obsession with young boys had begun already. But it was not in my mind when I went down to spend the summer of 1969 in a remote farm cottage on the Dorset–Wiltshire border. I had finished *A Change for the Better*, it was about to be published, and I wanted to start a new novel, but had no idea for one at all. I was in rather a panic because of that. I was only happy, only felt myself to be fully alive, in those days, when writing a novel. (I also had a publisher anxiously asking for another book from me, and I needed the money badly. Those are the three best spurs I know to the production of a piece of work; they provide the best incentive and the most favourable conditions for the right kind of idea, or 'inspiration' to appear.)

I had never been to the West Country, and I at once loved that very typical, rural corner of it, explored the fields and woods around my cottage, sat and watched deer feed in the evenings, stayed up all night watching for badgers, had a terrifying experience with a crow, one hot afternoon, read and fretted, and wandered about in that restless way a writer does when things are just starting to simmer deep inside him but aren't yet ready to boil over onto the page.

I'd got my setting, and settings are always very, very important to me, every bit as much as characters or themes. I have a strong sense of place, and this one gave off all the right vibrations, which struck answering chords deep in my imagination. Whenever I go to a place and this starts happening, it is as though I develop another sense, or else all my other senses become more acute – I see, hear, smell things more vividly and strongly, and there is an atmosphere which is partly real, partly made-up, so that I can't precisely tell which is the real place and which is the place within me, the one I am creating. I think this is often true, and why it is sometimes a disappointment to visit 'the real setting' of a novel. Hardy's Wessex, or Wordsworth's Lakes, or Lawrence Durrell's Alexandria, they are real. But they are also 'landscapes of the mind'.

So, I could take you to 'Derne', where there is a real Hang Wood, (called just that), and a 'Warings' (called something else), and a castle, a few miles away. But I doubt if you would get anything more out of the novel if I did – perhaps less; it is best imagined, recreated in your own mind, for this is one of the most important ways a reader works with the writer, lending him his creativity, giving as well as taking. A novel is a two-way process, something made by the reader as well as by the writer.

What happened to trigger off my novel was the arrival, on a week's holiday, of two eleven year-old boys at the farm – the grandson of the farmer, and his school-friend. I kept bumping into them about the countryside, though I didn't really talk to them, and they were certainly not Kingshaw and Hooper in any sense. Yet they were the start of Kingshaw and Hooper – without these boys, Charles and Toby, my two characters could never have been invented. That's how it happens, that's the answer to the question 'do you get your ideas and people from real life?' Some real-life incident is the essential trigger, and there may be tiny physical details of appearance which are copied down from the real-life model, but after that, invention, story-telling, the creative imagination, takes over completely.

The novel is about the two boys and about their relationship, in that claustrophobic house, and the countryside, where they are locked together for a summer, struggling, wrestling this way and that, moving towards a release, an escape, a parting, a conclusion and resolution. It isn't really about their parents, Mrs Kingshaw and Mr Hooper. They are rather two-dimensional characters, and deliberately so; they are formalised even in speech-style (whereas the boys talk, I hope, as eleven-year-old boys do talk). We are distanced from the adults, and do not go far inside their minds and emotions.

The 'normal' world is represented by Fielding; he fits, he can relate naturally, is at ease within himself, and therefore, with others, and perhaps he would be Kingshaw's escape-route, if they were to stay in the village, and not go off to separate schools; Fielding would teach Kingshaw, and be patient, befriend, make confident – in other words, be his salvation.

If that had happened, then *I'm the King of the Castle* would be a triumphant story, a comedy; not because it would be a funny book, but in the sense in which Shakespeare's comedies are comedies, with happy endings, in which the protagonists learn the truth about their real selves in time to start doing something about it; misfits find their rightful places and partners and the future stretches more hopefully ahead for all.

But this is a tragedy. The only peace and resolution Kingshaw can find is in death. And I cannot hold out much hope for the remaining trio achieving a contented family life, for Hooper becoming a mature, well-integrated, happy adult human being, given their respective personalities, and with the shadow of Kingshaw's suicide hanging over them all, forever.

(1981)

Strange Meeting

by Susan Hill

(Longmans Imprint Edition)

When I was a small child, we used to visit my maternal grandmother and her sister, a Great Aunt, who lived in another town. They had come from a large family, and used to talk about it to me sometimes. There were eight sisters altogether, including one, named Elizabeth, who came to a terrible end, burned to death when her nightdress caught fire as she lit the range early one morning. That story became engraved upon my memory. It still is.

But there was another one, too, which had almost as great an impact. The eight sisters had just one brother, cherished and idolised by them all, of course. When he was eighteen, he went to war – the Great War, as they called it, the 1914–18 War. On his nineteenth birthday, he was killed, like so many thousands of other young men, at the Battle of the Somme.

I don't think the family was ever the same again, nor so many families like it. He was a young man from a whole generation which was, quite simply, wiped out.

They had a photograph of him in his uniform, and I used to take it down and look at it. He had such a young face, even I could see that, as a child, he was not much more than a child himself. His ears stuck out, I remember, and his hair was cut very, very short under his cap. His Christian name was Sidney, and the family surname was Owen. It is a coincidence, of course, but the long arm of *that*, as they say, is a long one, and I am a believer in these small signs and symbols, as important parts of one's life.

He was an Owen, and so was Wilfred (no relation) the

greatest of that rich generation of poets who flowered to such quick maturity in the Great War. Later, I discovered another young soldier whose name was Owen – Owen Wingrave, hero of a Henry James short story, about whom Benjamin Britten wrote one of his operas. The magic circle joins hands, at that point, for it was Britten, the man whose work has had more influence upon mine than anyone else's (including other writers), who first brought me back to my memories of Great Uncle Sidney Owen.

In 1962 I went to a performance of Britten's *War Requiem*. I didn't know in advance much about what it was going to be like, or about, I only knew that what music of his I had already heard I had responded to at once, and that it had remained with me, in my mind and my heart, had fired my imagination. But I was not at all prepared for the effect that performance of the *War Requiem* was to have on me. I came out of it feeling dazed, as though something very important had happened – to me, I mean, as well as in musical terms – I can't easily explain it or even describe it. But one result was that I became filled with the desire to write something myself about the First World War. But not yet, not yet. I wasn't anywhere near ready.

For the next eight years, I did a lot of things, but all the time, on and off, I read books about that war, and thought about it a lot. Yet I kept on suppressing the desire to write about it, whenever it surfaced. To tell the truth, I was scared of the idea. How could I do it? What did I know? I hadn't been there, I only knew what I had read, and imagined.

But it wasn't the ability to absorb facts and re-create the past that I doubted, it was not the possibility of that kind of routine, practical failure that frightened me. It was the knowledge that I should have to sink myself completely and utterly in imagination, in emotions, into the experience of that awful war. In writing about it, I realised that a big piece of my own self would somehow disappear, I should never be quite the same again. The facts were horrible too, of course; I did not think I wanted to find out more than I already knew about the carnage, the human waste, the folly and the cruelty, the devastating suffering.

But if we are to grow – and I am sure that is what we are meant to do, that is the point of our existence – we must change, we have to learn things, and also give things up, and those things include the cosiness of ignorance and the safety of uninvolvement and personal detachment. To understand the present – which is where eternity is – to see what is good and recognise what is evil in order to fight and overcome it, we have to know it, face and accept it, and be hurt and personally changed, too, by various aspects of the truth.

Besides, I was over-dramatising. Heaven knows, I was only going to go through the trenches *imaginatively*, I would come out of them alive and well and sitting in my study! You couldn't say that about all those young men.

In 1969 and 1970 I wrote, in rapid succession, a novel called *I'm the King of the Castle*, a short novel, *The Albatross*, then several short stories and radio plays. I was, as it were, well run-in. I knew that now, if ever, was the time to tackle a novel about the First World War.

From the summer until Christmas, I read everything I could lay my hands on, in a rather unselective and haphazard way. I went to the London Library, where I found row upon row of memoirs, diaries, and letters by soldiers of the First World War, many of them privately printed by relatives, after the deaths of their young authors. I read volumes of autobiography, like Robert Graves's *Goodbye to All That*, and those of Siegfried Sassoon and Guy Chapman. I read the poets, major and minor, I read long official histories and biographies of the Kaiser and General Haig, I read one novel only, Remarque's *All Quiet on the Western Front*. I read until I could read no more. And as I did so, various things crystallised, by themselves, in my mind. I decided I would write about soldiers – as opposed to sailors or airmen – and in the trenches, not anywhere else. For it was the trenches that were the real, black heart of that war, between and in and around them so many died for so precious little ground. In them, the worst experiences were suffered, and the best of the poetry written. Also, it was going to be easier to find out about trench warfare and life, because it was really very limited and circumscribed.

After Christmas, 1970, I drove off to my rented fisherman's cottage in Aldeburgh – Britten's Aldeburgh; I had already worked there, happily and freely, in the two previous winters. It felt like home, to be beside that grey, North Sea and shingle shore, for I was born by the sea, a bit further up the same North-east coast, in Yorkshire.

Also, on the outskirts of the small town of Aldeburgh, there are marshes, crossed by dykes and they are flat, flat and wet under the wide sky. When it was grey and cold, those marshes took on something of the aspect of the fields of Flanders. Here and there, people had dumped old bicycle wheels and tin oil drums, and they had half-sunk into the mud, and rusty metal loomed up out of the pools of water, like the debris of a battlefield. When I took a break from writing, I walked on those marshes, early and late. In the end, I began to hear the boom of guns in the boom of the sea, and the cries of wounded men in the cries of the seagulls, to see blood, not the red of the early sunset, staining the water of the pools and ditches.

I had brought with me only a few out of the many books I had read; they were a comprehensive military history of the war, *The Somme* by Brigadier A. H. Farrar-Hockley, a small red handbook of regulations issued to officers of the British Army in 1914, and the *Collected Poems* of Wilfred Owen.

I cannot say, now, where my story within the story – that of the friendship between the two young soldiers, Barton and Hilliard – came from, though one personal relationship I had observed bore some resemblance to certain aspects of it. But all the details of their personalities and backgrounds, and the characters of the other soldiers, and the day-to-day details of what happened to them, all those came to me as I went along, each day, rising up into my mind ready-formed. This has always been my experience when writing fiction. It is no good enquiring too closely into the origins of it all, and I am slightly superstitious about doing so. I have learned, over the years, simply to trust the workings and productions of my subconscious and of my imagination.

I began the book in mid-January and finished it at the end of March. I didn't do anything else much, apart from write it, and think about writing it, and then eat, sleep, walk – and have nightmares. I was not interrupted at all. There was no telephone in the cottage and that year there was a postal strike. I had one or two kind friends who gave me a meal and a social evening now and then, and that kept me from going a bit potty.

Many people have asked me, since it was published, whether it wasn't a terribly difficult book to write. The answer is, no, and then again, yes. No, in the practical sense. As I have said, the information about the war was abundantly available and the facts were easy to grasp, because they were rather repetitive. I had a military historian to check on my details, when the book was finished, in case I had got details about things like guns, and arms discipline and so forth, wrong. To reconstruct the battlefields of the war, and life in the camps, and the hospitals, and conversations about it all, back in England, was really very straightforward.

But – was it difficult? Yes. It was, as I had expected and dreaded, a devastating subject to get involved in, a terrible world to enter, imaginately, an appalling business to be with young soldiers, day and night, in the trenches and in battle, in danger and fear and dirt. I felt exhausted, tense, horrified, depressed and angry the entire time. At the end, I felt drained. There was none of the usual burst of exhilaration and euphoria at completing a piece of work. I had done what I'd always known I would do, one day, and had laid some personal ghosts. That was all.

Now, I am occasionally sent books about the Great War, to read or comment on, or review. People ask me to talk about it, in public or in private, too. I don't. When I wrote the last words of the novel, I wanted to do what Hilliard did – look 'up and ahead'. I have never once wanted to look back. I don't think I ever will.

(1984)

The Cold Country and other plays for radio

by Susan Hill

(BBC Publications)

I was born in 1942, and mine was a generation of radio listeners. I did not see a television programme until 1953 (the Coronation), and my family did not own a set until the year I left home for University. These are facts, not proud claims from a member of the anti-television lobby. But for most writers, the better habits of a lifetime are laid down, and the imaginative influences which bear fruit in later years most strongly exerted, in childhood and adolescence.

An enormous number of factors go into the making of a novelist; I can identify some – growing up as the only child of older parents in an isolated northern seaside resort, learning to read very early and subsequently devouring books of widely varying content and quality, but in huge quantities. Other factors remain mysterious. But although I began as a radio dramatist some twelve years after writing my first novel, the step was not so much a forwards one, in a new and unfamiliar direction, as a 'backwards' one. I was returning to a medium not so much with as *in* which I grew up. Radio was in my blood, as television and the cinema have never been (which is why, on the few occasions I have worked in those media, I have found the going so hard). Certainly, the writing of radio plays is a challenge and an excitement, and I encounter new difficulties, as well as problems, with every piece. But I slipped into the medium as into an old glove, which seemed to have moulded itself long ago to the shape of my own hand,

and I am still surprised that I did not make use of it much earlier.

Inevitably, the radio programmes to which I listened when young were as varied in subject-matter and quality as the books I read, and my experience of drama began with the Toytown plays and serial adaptations of *Children's Hour*. There were some restrictions on the number of listening-hours I was allowed to put in, but although some programmes might be considered 'too late at night' for me to hear, there was no nonsense talked about any being 'too old' for me. (I read many books which made the deepest impression upon me, long before I might have been considered 'old enough' to understand them.)

I heard hundreds of radio plays and the majority, good as well as mediocre, passed in one ear and out of the other; only three remain vividly in my memory now. Two are classics of radio writing, and I have become more closely familiar with them, through repeated readings and hearings, in adulthood. But it was the first occasion of listening to them which stayed with me. I remember my own imaginative response – the world I created within me, to match the dialogue and sound-pictures, the faces I put to the voices of the characters. The initial experience of any work of art which is to prove increasingly significant for the rest of one's life seems always to be surrounded in memory, like a fly in amber, by highly personal, incidental details; so that I recall, for example, the pattern of the upholstery on the chair in which I was sitting, the contents of the sandwich I was eating, when I first heard *Under Milk Wood*, and Louis MacNeice's *The Dark Tower*. Moreover, a true response to any product of the creative imagination is a more individual matter than simple recognition of, and admiration for, the universally acclaimed masterpieces – which may be no more than an attitude of deference. One radio play which made not only an immediate impact upon me, as a young listener, but which has had a strong influence on my own work, was a Third Programme adaptation of Marghanita Laski's *Little Boy Lost*, starring Margaret Rawlings and produced in 1957. (I heard it only once and, unlike the Thomas and MacNeice plays, have never read any scripted version.)

I began to 'write' (in the sense of making up characters and weaving stories around them) almost before I learned to read, and my initial literary excursions were all dramatic. I made up puppet plays, epics for a cardboard toy theatre, nursery dramas – all parts acted aloud by me, and with dialogue and (scanty) plot improvised as I went along. But when I began to write seriously, I wrote prose – stories, and very soon, a novel. Plays became childish things, which I was anxious to put away when I aspired to be adult. It took someone else to lead me back into that early world of drama. I began my career as a radio playwright by a series of what, at the time, seemed mere chances and coincidences, but which, with hindsight, reveal themselves as one more pattern of divine guidance. Two novels of mine were adapted, with great skill, by Guy Vaesen, as plays for transmission on Radio 4, but my next book, *I'm the King of the Castle*, was unsuitable for translation to the air in dramatic form, and Guy (then a Senior Radio Drama Producer) suggested I write an original radio play. I was doubtful about the idea, but began work on *The End of Summer* the following week. It was a piece which wrote itself. At the time, I thought I was playing very safe by restricting myself to a length of sixty minutes, and to two main characters. In fact, this can be the most difficult format of all to follow; any faults stick out like sore thumbs, flagging invention and unconvincing dialogue are not glossed over, and the listener's attention held by the use of music, an assorted battery of sound effects, and a 'cast of thousands'.

The End of Summer is a beginner's piece, and its flaws are obvious to me now. Nevertheless, it does contain all the elements of which I was to make greater use in subsequent plays. There is music, and it is not merely incidental; the Schubert song, 'Frühlingstraum', is a leitmotif, and its words stimulate reactions, emotions and changes in the two characters, all of which are reflected in their conversation.

In the second volume of his autobiography, *At Home*, the late William Plomer noted that all writers have 'some unusual concentration of interest, some fantasy or obsession or predilection which has been an essential motive force in their work. It may be a passion for a person, place or thing . . .' Some of my own obsessions have been transitory, and I have worked them out, as basic themes or images, in a single book, story or play. Others are permanent, and I return to them, to find further inspiration. But I have never written anything which has not reflected one, or several, of these passions – they are far more than mere 'interests'. At the time of writing *The End of Summer* I was obsessed with the moon; ever since I sat in the garden of a remote Dorset cottage listening to the transmitted voices of the first men on the moon and looking, simultaneously, at the real moon in the sky, poetic, mythical and musical moon-associations had danced through my head. The moon has always been linked in men's minds – and hence, in their legends, superstitions and art – with water, and although my moon-infatuation proved temporary, my obsession with water, in all its forms, and with ideas of death by drowning is permanent. A psychoanalyst might make much – or little – of it; in either case, it is dangerous for an artist to delve too deeply into the sources of his principal fantasies, and the reasons underlying them.

Each of the radio plays in this volume deals with one, or more, of my passions. The absorption in young children, about whom I write constantly, was greatly stimulated by the Marghanita Laski play.

After *The End of Summer* I had more ambitious ideas. *Lizard in the Grass* developed one of my water-obsessions – the image of sunken and lost cities, whether fabulous (Atlantis, Avalon) or real. I had frequently walked along the cliffs above Dunwich, in Suffolk, imagining that once great and prosperous city and its inhabitants, long ago lost beneath the North Sea, and always half-expecting to hear the legendary sounding of church bells from the deep. Plays, like novels and stories, are formed by a process of accretion; ideas floating around in the writer's mind (or in odd notebooks) gradually come together. I went to a convent school on the East coast, and I was as rebellious and dreamy as the heroine Jane of *Lizard in the Grass*. I transferred my convent to the Dunwich cliffs, and then had two elements of a play. Since reading English at University, I had been intermittently fascinated by the work, character and certain events in the life of the sixteenth-century poet John Skelton. But it was a chance rereading of an essay about him by E. M. Forster (in his collection entitled *Two Cheers for*

Democracy), while I was mulling over the possible new play, which provided me with the final and most important element. Forster's essay, a masterly piece of evocation and analysis, led me to other books about Skelton, but I took great liberties with him, mainly by removing him from the inland town of Diss, in Norfolk, where he was Rector, and setting him down at Dunwich, at the time of the great storm which washed the town away. I also brought him into 'the present' by making him materialise from one of his bones, which Jane finds on Dunwich beach. I was learning that, in radio drama, one can do anything at all with the juxtaposition of events in time and space. *Lizard in the Grass* was not so much a difficult play to write as to organise – rather like fitting together a four-dimensional jigsaw.

There is a long and honourable tradition in radio drama of the use of specially composed music, and this was the first play in which Geoffrey Burgon collaborated with me, and with the producer, Guy Vaesen, to produce a setting of some lines of Skelton, for boy's treble voice and harp (a magical sound combination).

I had now written two quite distinct types of radio play. The small-cast, closed-circle kind, with minimal sound effects. And the multi-stranded, many-layered piece. I find that a dramatic idea fits, from the very beginning, into one or the other form, that each presents its own particular challenges, possibilities and problems, and that the radio medium can take both in its stride.

Ever since my imagination was fired by the accounts of the ascent of Everest, in 1953, I have been spasmodically obsessed with the cold, white, desolate worlds of the Arctic and the Antarctic, but I was not planning a radio play as I listened to Vaughan Williams's *Sinfonia Antarctica* one evening in 1970. However, ideas drop down from heaven, and clamour to be made immediate use of, and before the music was over I had been presented with four male characters (ready equipped with names) in a hopeless situation, stranded in a tent in a blizzard at the dead-end of some expedition. *The Cold Country* is another closed-circle play (though there is some rather clumsy use of flashback). This was one of the few occasions when I sat down to write and followed my nose; the theme and ideas unfolded one by one, as I began to wonder *why* men went on such forays, and to consider what tensions and conflicts the claustrophobic situation of these people would generate. I have often been suspicious of writers who claim that their characters 'take over', because I have always felt very much in control of a given piece of work. Yet in a sense it was Ossie, Chip, Barney and Jo who played out their own drama, and who decided their own fates.

The synopsis, on the basis of which *Consider the Lilies* was commissioned, hinted at the principal theme and characters – a middle-aged curator of a botanical garden who sees visions, and his relationship with a young, dying girl. But I had not clarified my own ideas sufficiently, and the first version of the play was a disaster; I had taken several wrong turnings, and the dramatic style clashed hopelessly with the inner themes. The final version emerged only after a hard struggle, and it was largely the result of guidance, suggestion and inspiration by Guy Vaesen, so much so that it ought to bear his name, as co-author. I had planned to use specially composed music again; mainly because it was the only way, in a sound medium, that I could suggest the nature of the botanist's visions of dancing angels and the light of God vibrating through plants and trees. But the idea of having two Plant Choruses (one chorus on each stereo speaker) came from Guy Vaesen; and the character of Lesage took on real life and depth and motivation only after he had taken him apart. My original Assistant-curator was a puppet-figure, all bad and black, just as the Curator was all good and white, but such over-simplifications do not have validity outside the structure and world picture of, say, a medieval morality play.

There was more collaboration to come. I had never gone into the studio during the recording of any of my plays; I felt that the presence of the author (even when sitting mute in the background of the control room) would inhibit producer and cast. But I was persuaded to go down for the production of *Consider the Lilies*, only to find that, especially in the final scenes, the actors were having great problems with the interpretation of their parts, because of faulty writing. After long talks with Tony Britton, Helen Worth and, again, Guy Vaesen, several scenes were rearranged, cut, or rewritten entirely in the margins of scripts, during lunch and coffee breaks. I still adhere to my rule that the author must not interfere in any way with the work of producer, actors or technicians, but I shall not be absent from studio during any future recordings, if only because a radio playwright's education is a continuing one, and a day spent listening and observing, in silence, can teach one more than weeks in the study with a script-in-progress.

Strip Jack Naked was originally conceived and written as a stage play, which, clearly, it is not, and there were very few alterations needed to fit it for its true medium. It is intended to be a stark piece which must, more than any of the other plays, stand or fall on the basis of its dialogue. The actors have to work extremely hard, there is no music, no use of flashback, sound effects are pared to a minimum, so that the three characters may emerge from cold.

Many people have asked the two questions, 'What can radio drama do? What can't it do?' Whenever I mull over them myself, I return to two quite simple, but comprehensive answers. They are, respectively, 'Anything' and 'Nothing'. Except, of course, for the obvious fact, that radio cannot produce an external visual image, as can the theatre, cinema or television. The visual images must be produced by each individual listener, in his own mind's eye. Radio plays demand the imaginative co-operation of the listener, he participates, he must work as hard, that is, as the conscientious reader of a novel, though he must not be aware that he is 'working'.

Although the audience for radio drama is large, it seems that people are finding it increasingly hard to listen to plays. Education is becoming more than ever dependent upon visual aids, and we live in a world of the fleeting television, cinematic and advertising image, a world in which our eyes are assaulted, whilst we remain passive. We are not being trained *how* to look, our visual awareness is not expanding – rather the reverse. Radio plays demand a patient attentiveness from the listener, but it should also, surely, be an expectant attentiveness. Radio may be, in many ways, a slower-paced medium than television, but the off-button can be depressed with as little effort (it is harder to leave a theatre in mid-act). The playwright may do anything – except *bore*.

Radio drama is flourishing and expanding, the technical resources available to the playwright are increasing, standards of production can be much higher than in many areas of the modern theatre, and of television, many of our finest actors specifically ask for opportunities to work in radio, because the challenge to them is enormous; if the medium shows up bad writing, perhaps it shows up bad acting even more ruthlessly.

But in the last resort, radio drama is not about technicalities. As a writer, I do not want the audience even to be aware of them, for the moment any of these devices become obtrusive, and the listener asks 'How is it done'? then the play goes out of the window. Plays are about human beings in confrontation – with one another, and with various aspects of their own selves, the contents of their minds and hearts, their pasts, their fears and hopes for the future, the exigencies of their particular situations at given moments in time. When the last word has been said about 'the medium of radio', the most vital words have yet to be spoken; by the writer, through his character, to the listener – person to person. That is all.

(1975)

Radio Plays

CHANCES

Two Radio Monologues

First Broadcast in 1981

PART 1. THE GIRL

Place. On a cliff top above the sea. Fade up, from far below, the wash of a calm sea, and the occasional shout of a child playing on the beach. The girl comes up and sits down on the grass during the opening lines. She comes from Southern Ireland.

THE GIRL: Now isn't that a lovely thing, that sun on the water and the people enjoying themselves? Would you look at that? And I don't begrudge them, not at all. Those little children, all naked . . . our Mam would never have . . . Never.

(*She lies back*)

Ah, there now.
I didn't think I'd ever get up here this morning, I thought you'd have given up and gone. This man. One of the commercials. He had freckles all over his head, his scalp . . . underneath, where the hair was going thin . . . you notice things like that . . . I do. And he wanted three eggs. Three. So I got him three. And I come back with the three eggs and he said, 'Sunny side up, did I not say', which he did not, 'I want them sunny side up, take them back', so back I go, and we're two short this morning. Carol again. Headache. Do you ever get headaches? I never get them.

Ah, that sun on your face, isn't it wonderful? You'd go mad if you couldn't get somewhere. I would. All those rooms. Every day. Sometimes it comes to me . . . I'll sit on a bed in one of those rooms, and think, I'll give it up. I'll have to. I suddenly see myself, how I really am. Cleaning bedrooms out, up and down stairs, thump, thump, thump along corridors.

Until I'm grey.

My ankles get swollen now sometimes. I noticed that. This used to be a very classy town, did you know that? You'd never have got the commercials in those days, never. In those days . . . But it's not really a bad hotel.

I sat on this bed . . . it had an orange cover . . . shiny . . . I thought, what am I doing, what future is there in it? Only it's a very good place to be, just here, just now, in the sunshine.
And to be handy for Michael.

There's not a cloud. Not one. Think of the places you could be. Some terrible places. Like poor Sean. But you're the only person I could say I'd talked to since I got here. Truly talked to, not just 'Eggs or sausages? Going to be a lovely day again'. If it wasn't for coming up here to meet you, I'd be really lonely. There's work. And then you lean out of the window sometimes, at night, wishing. And then, you get so tired.

(*She sits up*)

Oh, there's a boat, right out there now, just one boat by itself, isn't that pretty? Like in picture books. Sailing on the water, like a cup and saucer. That's the kind of thing you want your mind to save up, for later.

You'd think I'd talk to Michael when he comes. Anyone would be right to suppose that. Michael isn't much of a real talker. They work so hard on those ferries, never stop, he gets tired, though he never complains. The money's good. Not bad.

I'd been reading in one of the bibles, sitting on that bed, when it came to me, how it was really a funny sort of life.

Pulling sheets, rinsing basins, setting tables for eggs or sausages. And not even in my own home for my own family, where it's what you'd be expecting to do.

I don't care to slip into too much thinking as a rule. Perhaps it was that bible? They have them in the lockers, every room has one. They're given. I just picked it up and opened it. It's true what they say about us. That we never read our bibles. You just hear bits, in the Mass. If you go to Mass. But never to sit down and read it.
'When a man hath taken a wife and married her, and it comes to pass that she find no favour in his eyes, because he hath found some uncleanness in her, then let him write her a bill of divorcement and give it in her hand and send her out of his house. And when she is departed out of his house, she may go and be another man's wife'.
Well I was never ever told there were such things as that in the bible. It'd make you start asking all sorts of questions wouldn't it? If you was to sit down and read it through like any other book?
'And I looked and behold, a pale horse, and his name that was on him was Death, and Hell followed him'.
It did frighten me, sitting there. I thought after a bit, maybe it's all for the best that they don't encourage us to read it so much, maybe they *do* know the truth. It doesn't do to think too much.

Michael never thinks.
So I can't talk to him. His mind's all sealed up, can you understand? He was born like that, his father and his grandfather, they're like that, and all his brothers and his uncles. And my brother Sean. It makes me furious, I get really furious with him. He knows what he thinks about everything, and that what he thinks is the right thing to think, his mind's always sealed up and never will admit a chink of light. You might wonder how a person could be like that.
Oh, now there's another boat. Behind the first.
Cups and saucers. Is the tide going out or coming in? I never can tell that.
Swiss. Swish.

That's a lovely place for the little children, down there by those rocks, all covered in pinky weed. I'd have loved to be in a real place like that, when I was a little child. Little pools. Sometimes the water in those pools is colder than the sea itself. If you put your hand in it takes your breath. The sun never strikes it.
I go down there sometimes. Just to sit. I took Michael one evening. 'Just smell the smell' I said to Michael, 'Just smell it'. It's a green smell. Cold and green. He didn't take to it.

He's a very good looking person, you know. Michael. I think he is. And none of it is his fault. I wouldn't want you to think that. He can't help the way he was reared at home. He'd fight for me, do you know that? He's very good. He's very kind. He'd give me anything, anything at all. If he had it. He's come off the ferries some weeks, with his money in his pocket, and that's money he's worked for, day and night shifts, and it's terribly stormy sometimes and still they have to work, and he's said, 'Here you are, you have that, you keep it, it's too much trouble to me. You do what's best with it, you put it away safe. Or buy yourself something. Anything, I don't care'. And he really doesn't. So long as he's got a pound or two for his drink and his smokes, and maybe a newspaper. And he likes a chocolate bar. That's how I mean, kind.
It worries me. Because I don't think a man should be like that, do you? Just handing his wages over. 'You have that, you take charge of that for me'.
That's like his Mammy always did.
Well, I won't be his Mammy.

There's times when I let myself see the truth. I know how things would turn out.
Shall I tell you how I first found out? It was at Eileen Noonan's wedding. Eileen Noonan was the girl of a friend of Mam's. Very pretty. Well, well, quite pretty. But big, a great big girl, to see her walking down the street you'd even feel sorry for her, yet she had no difficulty getting a man that would marry her, none at

all. I liked Eileen Noonan. She'd stop off on her way home from work, with maybe a heavy bag of shopping too, and lean it against the wall, and play with us, twosie ball, or french skipping, whatever was the craze, and we all went to her wedding, it was a grand occasion, it was just like you dream for, as a wedding day, with the sun shining and the flowers, and everybody slapping each other round the shoulders who hadn't spoken for fifteen years. I had a new frock. New to me. We all had something new. And then, you should have seen the hall, and the table piled high, and the drink and the dancing. There was a fiddler, and Eileen's cousin with the accordion, and the schoolteacher from St Joseph's sang 'This is my lovely day' and the sun shone and shone. He was a good man she was marrying, they all said, though he had two black teeth right in the front and one of them was broken and that spoiled him for me. I went off to find the lav. It was down a corridor and a couple of steps, at the back, and I came round this corner and there she was. It was where they hung their coats, the caretaker and all, and there was some pegs and a washbasin and a wooden bench, and there she was. She'd a beautiful dress. Maybe I wouldn't think it was now, only when you're younger, you think a wedding dress should be frills all up and down, as many as can be fitted on, don't you? I've changed in that respect.

She was like an angel to me that day. The dress and the pure white flowers and her face shining, like someone in a holy picture. She wasn't just Eileen Noonan.

She was crying her eyes out. Not dainty crying, her nose was running with it, and she was scrubbing her fists into her eyes. She never saw me. She never knew I'd been there at all, I've never told anyone else, never, from that day until now, not a soul. It wouldn't have been right.

And she came back from her honeymoon and lived in the next street and she was just like anybody else, and she still stopped to play with us, once in a way. Till she

had her own babies. And we were growing out of street games by then.
Her man had his teeth out in the end, so there was a great hole, which if anything was worse than before. Why couldn't he do better than that? It made me furious to see him not bother.

After that I didn't think about them anymore.

She was crying as though her heart was broken and I just crept away and went to the lav, and sat on there and thought it all out. What it meant.
'Would you look at yourself with a face like a wet week' our Dad said. 'Would you condescend to give them a smile and a wave or have you a pain in the you-know-where?'

They were going off. She had a lilac suit and they were going to Shannon airport for a plane, which was a very big thing in those days, it wasn't ten a penny as it maybe is now, and everybody had had too much drink and it wouldn't be long before they'd go back inside and have more and then the fighting would start like it always did and we kids would be sent home. The sun had shone all day. But it stuck in my throat to shout and laugh and wish them luck and kiss everybody for miles around. Though I stared right deep into her eyes. Eileen Quinn she was now, and you'd never have told she'd been sobbing. So perhaps it was nothing.
It wasn't nothing.

I've come here to be handy for Michael, why else would I be here?
But I know how it would turn out. Whether he gave me all his wages every week or kept them to himself. Living at the back of his Mam's or our Mam's, or in two rooms that weren't our own – that would be if we were very, very lucky. And the babies and him never at home or else at home too much of the time, and the babies getting coughs and colds and you tied hand and foot to them and the love you love them with, for the rest of your days.

I should be grateful for Eileen Noonan's crying.

Look at the sea.

There's the rest of the wide world, and what could there be for me to do in it? Tell me that if you can.

I'd like to see into my future. But I'd be afraid to.

Today I think, I just do not know how it will be. But today is a good day. Because of the sun on that sea and the little boats. And talking to you gives me a lot of satisfaction.

Most days I do know how it will be and no use pretending.

But the only thing for certain is, one day I'll be dead. I wake up in the night and I wonder when and where I'll die and my heart almost jumps out of my mouth for the fear of it.

I was thinking what you said. About me going straight there, straight to the point. You said, 'When you've something to say, you say it, when there's a truth to be told, what's in your head or heart you tell it'. You said. I remember that.

Do you know what I'd love? I'd love a cup of coffee and a cake, brought me on a tray, with one of those lace doilies and a silver spoon and the sugar like little chips of glass. And to eat the cake with a fork.

But it's great to see the sun. I'm the lucky one, I know that. There's poor Michael, on the long shift, crossing back, so it's nearly morning by the time they're all cleared up and he's to start again at three.

Sometimes, Mam gets a kitchen chair and sits at the street door, to get a bit of the evening sun. You'd think it'd be easier, with only Paul left there, but it's not so, she says, it's as bad as ever it was, two men at home and never lift a finger and us girls not there to help any longer.
It's dragging your legs about like weights, she says,

because you're older. She looks older.

She misses Sean.

If I think at all about that day I went to see Sean, I could either shout or weep. If I close my eyes now, and wish, I wish to open them and have him here with me, getting the pleasure of the sun and all. Seeing the little boats.

The old Sean.

It was never meant to be Sean that was going for a priest. That was to be Patrick. But Patrick lost his faith and packed his bags when he was not yet eighteen and came to England, for a soldier. They wouldn't take him, his eyes were poor.

He's got a wife now, and no work. He doesn't write home. Out of shame, Mam says. I ought to go and see him. But it was Sean I saw, in that terrible place.

Oh, there was one summer when we were so happy. Some fishing friend of Dad's cousin Eddy knew of a farm. We went in the old car, the lot of us all scrambled in together. A week, we went for. It could have been a lifetime. The smell of this grass just reminds me of it, if I press it down so, with my hand. And out of the open window, if it's warm at night.
That's how I like to think of us, as though we were all still there in that place, and I could go back to it. To us.

Sean was the happiest of all. He'd run all over the fields without his shoes and wave his arms in the air. 'You're crazy'. He was. And wouldn't give two sticks for anyone.

That was the old Sean.

Not now. 'Run away from this place', I said that day. 'Run, Sean'. But he'd lost the heart even to think of it.

He smokes cigarettes the whole time, one, then another, his fingers are yellow and brown with it. I hated the way he smelled. The whole house smelled.

I went there on the train. You don't see a green thing, not a tree, not one bit of grass, even the places where they kick the football or have an old slide and a swing are worn down to the brown earth, even the parks where the old people sit on the benches.

'How can you stay here?' I said.
'It's where I was sent', Sean said, in that voice I hate, that voice isn't his. 'I don't have the say'. And then, 'I've a mission to the people here', he said. 'They're good people. The place is important'.

But I could see his eyes. The way he looked round that brown room. He's gone thin, with the work and the smoking.

It's a little house and the parish priest is fat as lard, and he has a glass cabinet in his sitting room just packed full of the most beautiful crystal, glasses and vases and dishes and bowls. He took a key off a chain, and opened it. He took out a crystal vase. 'Put your hand to that', he said.

And Sean's room isn't so big but it feels big, with just the lino and the crucifix and those black suits.
There's a little bare garden and a privet hedge and you hear the traffic the whole time, you couldn't sit out there in the sun.

There's a housekeeper. 'Yes, father, no father, kiss your arse for you father'.

It was to be Lent the week after. Sean was dreading Lent. He'd to give up his smoke.

'I hope you keep the faith', he said to me. I wanted to scream at him. I wanted to shake him, to let out the old Sean.

I said, 'Do you remember the farm, and the hayloft and how I saw those two horses shot dead in the field and it was you I came running to? Do you remember taking the boat out onto the lake and saying, "I'll lose us, we'll vanish, just you and me"?'

He wouldn't talk about it, he wouldn't look in my face. 'I don't remember', he said, and that was a lie. Then a woman came knocking at the door, wanting to make a confession and he'd to go.

He has a little car but I don't think he gets any pleasure from it. I sat in it. It smelled of the cigarettes. He'll smoke himself to death.

He's my favourite brother. And it wouldn't matter, not any of it, if it was meant for him, if I'd seen the light shining there in his eyes, like I've seen it in others, to show he believed. But it was never any of it for Sean. He went for a priest in place of Patrick, to please our Mam.
'It'll be alright', he said, the day he was packing for the seminary. 'It'll come out right.'

It's as wrong as it could be.

I hate them all.

There now, I've said it.

Do you see where the boy with the red bucket is going away up the beach? Do you see the line of his footprints, shining wet? Oh isn't that pretty? He can't see them. He's going to fill his bucket, maybe for a starfish. Only we can see his footprints like that, right up here.

Do you like my bracelet? Have I shown it to you before? 'You get yourself something', says Michael on my birthday. But he wouldn't go and choose it himself and wrap it up and all, make it a surprise. That's what I'd like.

I went and chose it myself.

It's a very nice bracelet.

But it's not the same.

That's how it always is. That's how it would always be, isn't it?

Disappointments.

Dad comes in and drops his boots right in the doorway, all caked with mud or else wet through and they don't smell exactly like the new-mown hay and Mam has always to bend down and pick them up and put them in their place, and I say 'Don't do it, why should you, don't put up with him'. And she says 'Anything's better than a lonely old age.' I can't make up my mind about that.

So I'm here because of Michael.

There's much worse places than the hotel to be working. I'd rather that than a shop. It's more homely.

I like to talk to you. So long as I can come up here sometimes and talk to you, I feel alright. Most of the time.

Isn't that sun really warm now? Isn't it a beautiful day? There's a lot more boats to see. Little white boats.

Ah, now it's coming in, the tide. You can tell that now, those footprints are all filling up with water.

You have to enjoy whatever you can.

Soon you won't see that line of footprints at all.

Today's a good day.

You have to make the most of the good days.

They aren't so many.

I never thought I'd get up here at all this morning, you've got to remember that.

Isn't that sunshine beautiful?

This is what I'll remember.

This is like those hayfields in summer and Sean going crazy in his bare feet.

I'll say, there was this. I'll be able to say that much.

Isn't that sunshine beautiful?

(*The sea washes in and out, the children call*)

PART 2. THE WOMAN

THE WOMAN: And the luggage just sat there. Anyone might have tripped over it. The girl went back to her typewriter. In the office, behind the glass. The luggage just sat there. It seemed as if we were expected to carry it ourselves. No one offered. Oh, there are changes every year, the hotel isn't what it was. In the old days. But there has always been someone to carry the luggage.
I slipped my coat off, it was so warm. He gets so irritable, over things like that. He can be so very rude. People don't like it. I'm used to it. The way he speaks to me.
Over forty years . . . But other people don't like it.

If I turn my back, and watch the front door, the people coming in and out . . . or watch the promenade, out of that window . . . I needn't watch him. His jowls go red like a turkey wattle.

I needn't watch.

They took the bags. In the end. A girl took them. Three flights of stairs but she almost ran. Neat figure. Ah. 'No trouble at all', she said, and almost ran up.
There used to be a porter. There used to be a boy in a uniform cap, looked old, he had an old wizened face, so that you were never sure if he was a boy or not. The children used to laugh. Oh, thirty years ago.

And you put your shoes outside the door at night, for cleaning.

She was Irish.
He'll have walked well behind her, trying to see up her skirt, round the bends in the staircase.

I like to watch the people on the promenade. I like the minutes alone.

All changed, he says, and of course . . .
All made a muck of.
It doesn't trouble me very much.

I live in a room inside.
A sand coloured car pulled onto the forecourt, with a man's jacket hanging up on a peg beside the driver's seat. He said, 'See that. Commercial traveller'. Gibbering. There were never under any circumstances cars on the front of the hotel. You stopped and got out, if you had a car, and then it was taken round the back, with the luggage. To the service entrance. I wish his teeth were better fitting, just at the side.

Little things. Easy to attend to. Personal things. Courtesies, my mother said, these little courtesies about bodily matters, make so much difference. Consideration. Living together. Your father, she said, had impeccable habits. Consideration. Remembering to close the lavatory door when you go in.

Of course, it is perfectly true, there would never have been commercial travellers here. In the old days.
But in our room, there is a wardrobe I'm sure I remember. And the same view of the sea and the promenade.

'Ah, I'll run up with them for you, don't you worry, won't take a moment. Sure, it's no trouble at all'. And she was friendly. Familiar, even.

The staff were never familiar.

It was always like a play. I seemed to be on a stage. Different parts, and now, well, an old woman. But it has been a way to get by. To be in a play, so that none of it is ever real, and cannot touch me. Or hurt me.
I stay inside my room, with the door closed. I lock it. No one comes in.

He never came in.

But then, life slipped by and somehow . . . there should be something more. Something real.

When he comes down, we'll have tea.
In our room, there's a kettle, and cups and saucers, with tea or coffee, in little bags, and sugar and powdered milk, for convenience.
It's rather fun.
But I should prefer tea on a tray now.
And the sun has come out, after all.

Perhaps he will try to press against her, going into the room. Brush against her. His shoulder near to her breast. But the Irish were always very strict.

The evening is best here. I like the evening.

But when the children were small, it was the early mornings. Leaving him in bed, and going down on to the sand after the tide had gone right out. It was hard and flat and wet. It shone. Everything clean. And little boneless sea creatures in the cold rock pools. Dark pools.

The first sun shone on their waiting faces. Then I stood still and then, oh, unlock the door, creep out, look, the sun, the new day. Come very softly, tell no one. Like the crab and the whelk, peering out of the shell.
Sometimes, with the children, in those early mornings, it was real, I would dare to come out of my room. There used to be a man with a moon face sweeping the gutters with a wet brush.
And we looked back at the line of our footprints. We are the first people, at the dawning of the world, Roger said.

I was terrified of my children. I looked into their faces, searching, and they looked back, knowing. They knew so much more than I did. Knew the answers and the rules of the game. I shivered when they looked back. I closed my door and went inside.

On the stage, the lights came up. Bright sunlight. A morning.

Let's run back, let's get a starfish, let's shout, let's have ten sausages for breakfast, let's go and jump on him. Run, run, run. They ran.

Tch tch. There's no bell to ring. There used to be a small brass bell on every table. For service. It's not the same. I look the part. A little lace at the collar and a seed pearl brooch, the correct number of wrinkles, if they were to glance across they would see I look the part, they would say, 'That lady will be waiting for tea'.

But in the evenings, it could have been the South of France. Almost. The play was more fashionable and I never came out of my locked room. But I liked the evenings.
My heart used to pound with excitement, I touched the skin of my own neck and arms as I changed, there was the smell of scent and the feel of light silk, the cold of a heavier bracelet on my wrist. I twirled in front of the mirror, I liked this act of the play.
The children went to bed. Of course we always brought Angeline. Did she mind, evening after evening? Did she creep down and talk in whispers in the shadows to someone's driver. The porter by the door?

People went walking out in the summer evenings, just a shawl slipped over the shoulders, it really was a promenade. Doors were open onto gardens, and pools of light were on the flowers, the paths. Insects danced. It seemed romantic. I could pretend. People smiled, half nodded. It was all couples. Arm in arm. I scarcely minded that. And the lights of the harbour twinkled. It was always warm. In the next hotel, there was a small orchestra, a few couples danced. I wanted to go in. Cocktails in triangular glasses. Cheap, he said. The pianist wore a cream jacket. He was older than he pretended. He'd play anything you wanted. People called out. 'A Nightingale Sang In Berkeley Square.' 'Blue Moon.' His eyes were miles away, he was smiling, smiling, like a dummy, smiling into the darkness, at nothing. Playing on. There was the promise of something in the air then. I held my breath. I listened. But I never unlocked my door. I only walked about in a dream on that stage. Arm in arm.

She wasn't here last year. After a while, the Irish girls seem the same. But she wasn't here. Mrs Dolamore, she was the housekeeper, and the head waiter was Swiss. Oh, year after year.

When Roger was nine, he said at lunch in the dining room, 'Send this fish back, this fish stinks'.
Two little children, tottering towards me, laughing, arms out to me. Then running the other way. His father's son. I never knew them. Even when they were babies, somehow. You're like the pig, I thought, looking down at Joan. I felt as if a great storm had been raging over me hour after hour, and in the morning, it had rolled away, the tide had gone out, carrying my body with it. Leaving a shell. Clean as a bone. And this baby in the blanket, snuffling through her nose. Tiny eyes. Like Alice's pig, I said. Even then.
'Send this fish back'. I thought I was going to faint with shame. We were sitting at a table in the bay window, and it was raised up on a little dais of its own. 'This fish stinks'. Another stage, and the audience staring up, shocked. 'Boy's learning anyway', he said. But oh, I stayed deep in my room. Like the storm. It will pass, I said, this will pass. It passed.
They brought another plate of fish.
I was afraid of the cleverness in that boy's face.

When the girl lay in the bed and looked down at her baby and said 'Like the pig' from inside my locked room I said 'Mother!' 'Mother!' I said to the girl, mockingly.

'There, there, there. What is it? What's the matter? Don't cry. There, there'.
Those were my lines.

When he comes down, then we'll have tea. He can ask, he can rap on the reception desk. But he'll want to go for a walk, see the changes. 'Look at that. Place goes down every year. Look at the charabancs. Come on. Look what they've done over there. Look at that.'

There are always one or two people, you can find someone to talk to. Not too friendly but . . . That woman in the green and cream. Home counties, our sort of people, our age. Lines are drawn and we stay within them. I needn't leave my room. She has had her tea.

But once, he slept and snored, and I slipped out. Just once. It was very late, and I went down the promenade onto the foreshore by the boats. I went alone.
There were different smells down there. Frying fat and beer and the sugar of the doughnut stalls. Tap-tap, very high heels, and the girls leaned on the arms of sailors. Nobody knows who I am. Who am I? Who knows? I said.
I looked into their faces, and they knew things, too, but they'd have been glad to share. They'd laughed, they shrieked with laughter, kiss me quick, they said, and did, in doorways and behind the low sea wall. Fumbling fingers, and stroking, and soft moans and cries, with the sound of the sea, and I looked and listened, secrets.

Hello, sweetheart, all alone?
No, no, not that, I knew that, what I wanted was not that. Was . . .
Ah.
I ran.
But even now, if I open the window at night, if I close my eyes . . .
Even now.

Our room. Our bed. He snores and grunts. He has a fat neck. But I can live inside my own room. Locked away.

And after all, I was chosen, I was picked out. One girl from so many. He had plenty to choose from. I knew it was the only way I could live.

That woman. She's very smart. The green and cream is smart. Good shoes, good bag. And a neat ankle, he'd say. But no ring, after all. He chose me and he didn't have to. When I was a child of ten I prayed to be chosen.

To be here alone, with the nice Irish girls feeling sorry for you, saying, 'Go on, spoil yourself, have another egg. You're fancy free, go on', and they've all got young men and babies to come. I wouldn't want to be alone, not daring to look up.

I stood waiting to go to the church, and my dress felt stiff and my face was stiff, and the shoes pinched. My hair was tight. I peered out of the window of my locked room inside and saw a bride in white, with a white skin. For a moment I didn't recognise . . . But I loved that play, and the presents, the cutlery and the china and the linen and the glass. The young couple. Everybody waving. I was safe.
And a room of my own with a key.
I could never be alone.

I'm used to the way he speaks to me. I can ignore it. He's a fool, and mean over small amounts of money. But not a bad man.

The signs here used to be so discreet, they were painted in gold on dark wood. Lounge, cloakroom, reception, staff. Now there are green lights. Bar snacks. There was never a bar. There are lights all over the town, and so much fun, so much pleasure, there are trips on the gaudy little boat at night. The children used to whine and bicker with each other, after three days they were bored. Dig in the sand, splash in the sea. Fresh air. Explore the rock pools. 'Those children in blue shorts are *common*', Roger said.

Ah, may I have a pot of tea, china tea with lemon, and some plain biscuits? It's too late for tea then.

They have such fresh bright faces and they are willing girls, they are nice girls. Friendly. The Irish girls always have good skins. They save their tips. Saving to get married, saving for rainy days. Saving to run away.

It's not a good life. Cleaning the rim of his shaving soap

off the wash basin, pulling off the pillowcases stained by the grease of our hair, drawing back curtain after curtain, 'Good morning, lovely morning'.

He will have gone to sleep. He will be lying on the bed with his shoes off.
In India that year, I wanted to talk to Indians. In the streets, in the market, on the trains. That was a marvellous play, bright and noisy, a crowded stage.
'India stinks', Roger said, and to the Ayah, who nodded and smiled and bowed to him, so that he slapped his hands with delight.

'India stinks, India stinks', he cried, and she shouted too, something in her own tongue, and laughed, and he laughed, at the appalling, cruel joke she couldn't share.
India stinks.
The boy's right. He said.
No tea.
But there is a kettle in the room.

If she looks up again, I may smile. But perhaps it's too soon. Too familiar. We have only just arrived. Perhaps tomorrow, we shall nod, as we go in to breakfast.
When he wakes, he will be irritable, and then want to walk. I used to walk in the sand without shoes. Sit on the rocks. Years ago.
Why not go? Before breakfast, very early.
There will be a man walking a brown dog, and a machine spraying the gutters, grinding along. A few children. The sea far, far out, a line of silver. The moon fading down. Put your finger into the centre of a sea anemone in the cold rock pool and the tentacles close and harden and tighten. You shiver.
The weed smells green and you lick the salt from your lips.
Why not?
Why not?
And the Irish girl will slip in with the morning tray and open the curtains. Lovely morning, and he will grunt and she will turn and he could have her, there, quick on

the bed, and afterwards, money, notes, money to save for a wedding, for the house, for the rainy day. Money to run away.
And on the beach I would stand in the pale sun.
Bare feet. Cold sand.

Unlock my door. Look outside. Safe. Now! Creep out carefully. Out of my shell, out of my locked room, into the sun. No one will see. Into the morning. Onto the sand, by the beautiful sea. And run, and run, and run. Leave them all. The empty house. The shell. The room. The bare bones washed clean and fetched up on the beach by the sea.
Go, go, run and run.
In the early morning.
Leave the old woman.
Run.

(*The sound of the sea, comes*)

THE END

AUTUMN

A Play for Radio

First Broadcast in 1985

Eva *is kneeling down, counting out bulbs.*

EVA: Sempre Avanti . . . Carbiner . . . Ice Folly . . . Mount Hood . . . Beersheba . . . Lent Lily . . . Cheerfulness. . .

TOM (*coming up*): Tea.

EVA: Oh . . . my back. . .

TOM: Here.

EVA: No, wait a minute. (*Gets up*) There.

TOM: You shouldn't be sitting on the grass.

EVA: It's as dry as chalk. Too dry.

TOM: Yes. My lawn . . .

EVA: Oh, your lawn . . .

TOM: Come and sit down.

EVA: Yes.

(*They sit.*)

I bought ten dozen, but I don't think there can be enough.

TOM: Enough for you to try and plant all in one afternoon.

EVA: There ought to be hundreds.

TOM: They'll spread.

EVA: At Haven Top there were . . . oh, thousands . . . great white drifts of flowers . . .

TOM: Yes. Your tea?

EVA: Yes.

TOM: There's plenty of time for everything.

EVA: But they ought to be in by the middle of October.

TOM: And it is only the middle of September.

EVA: And then there are the tulips.

TOM: 'Make that the tulips may have share
Of sweetness, seeing they are fair.'

EVA: So much to do . . . look at it . . . so little done.

TOM: They did little enough.

EVA: And that little was hideous. How could people have lived here . . . *here* . . . for twenty seven years and simply not had eyes to see. They saw nothing. They didn't care.

TOM: Well, we're here now. Look upon it as a rescue.

EVA: Poor old house. Poor garden.

TOM: Drink your *tea*.

EVA: When I was having a rest from planting . . . I looked up . . . I looked around and I saw apple trees . . . I saw an orchard, Tom . . . over there . . . perhaps two or three dozen trees? And flowers growing up through the grass beneath.

TOM: Yes. I like that idea.

EVA: Oh, planting trees is a business . . . you need to do it in the autumn . . . well, November . . . we ought to start ordering . . .

TOM: There's plenty of time.

EVA: Yes, but . . .

TOM: Give yourself time, Eva. We've plenty . . .
(EVA *is crying*.)
Oh now . . . don't . . . you've been fine, this has been the best afternoon for a long time . . . don't, now . . .

EVA: There's no point in any of it. What have I been talking about. There is no *point*.

TOM: You know there is.

EVA: Why did we come here at all? What are we doing all this for. Planting a garden . . . looking into the future and seeing . . . an orchard, for God's sake!

TOM: Yes. That's right.

EVA: How can we bother?

TOM: We might have a few sheep. I'd like that . . . grazing in among the apple trees.

EVA: It's all for nothing.

TOM: No, it is for us. We have to do it. You know that. You've said so yourself . . . we have to, Eva.

EVA: It's like running round in circles, or talking very fast for a long time, about nothing very much . . . keep busy, keep busy . . . we've come here to keep busy haven't we? My God, look at us! Won't it be wonderful? This place . . . we'll never have a spare moment, there'll be no excuse at all not to keep busy . . . we'll never stop.

TOM: Good.

EVA: We should have stayed there.

TOM: Oh no.

EVA: It would have been more . . . honest.

TOM: I couldn't have stayed there another week.

EVA: You've stopped feeling.

TOM: All right. Perhaps I have. Perhaps you should do the same.

EVA: What are you saying?

TOM: A new start. This is a new life for us. Here. You agreed on it.

EVA: But it was wrong. There's no new start and no new life. Those things can't happen.
(*Silence.*)

TOM: Your tea is cold.

EVA: Yes.

TOM: There's a chill in the air now . . . just a touch of mist . . . I felt it this morning, too. Yet in the middle of the day, it's still summer. But it isn't summer.

EVA: Conkers and sycamore wings . . . see? Bunches of ash keys. Great drifts of leaves.

TOM: Bonfires.

EVA: Oh, your bonfires.

TOM: 'Now is the time for the burning of leaves.'

EVA: Your poetry.

TOM: I wish you had . . . something. Well . . . look at all the bulbs you've planted . . .

EVA: Are you going to pat me on the back?

TOM: I'm glad you did it. That's all.

EVA: When he was a little boy . . . about seven, I suppose . . . he made such a stack of leaves . . . like a great pyre . . . for you to burn.

TOM: Yes.

EVA: Once he collected two hundred and eighty-seven

conkers in a single weekend. They were all in a cardboard carton under his bed. They stayed there for weeks. They went very small and shrivelled. I threw them out then.

TOM: Yes.

EVA: She never bothered. Girls don't. Why don't they?

TOM: I don't know.

EVA: I can see them, Tom.

TOM: No.

EVA: Yes. Even here. It doesn't make any difference, you know. They're in this house, and in this garden. They've come with us. Nothing has changed.

TOM: It has to change.

EVA: Their voices whisper in my ears. Don't you ever hear them? Haven't you seen them?

TOM: No!

EVA: What's wrong with you? When they whisper, I can feel their breath on my face. It smells sweet as hay. Their faces peer into mine. They peer into my dreams. When I'm on my own in the house, I can hear them both upstairs, laughing. If I'm out here, in the garden, and I glance over my shoulder towards the house, I see them at the windows.

TOM: Let them go. If you let them go, all these . . . things you see . . . they'll fade.

EVA: But I don't want them to fade. It's all I have left.

TOM: Is it?

EVA: They'll be with me till the day I die.

TOM: And is that what you want?

EVA: Yes. Oh yes.

(*Silence.*)

TOM: You ought to pack the bulbs away, if you've finished. Put them back in their bags. Do you want me to help you? You can do the tulips tomorrow. It won't rain.

EVA: Yes.

TOM: I might sand the lawn. It needs sanding. I don't think they bothered. I shall enjoy having a new lawn to bring up to the mark!

EVA: You were always shouting at them for damaging the lawn. They used to be quite afraid of you.

TOM: So you told me.
EVA: How many times a day do you think about them, Tom? A dozen times? Fifty times?
TOM: Some days . . . I don't think of them at all. I've forgotten. Unless . . . something reminds me.
EVA: I remind you.
TOM: Yes.
EVA: I never stop thinking about them. They're there . . . all the time. Even when I'm not seeing them.
TOM: Tell them to go away.
EVA: Oh, I couldn't do that.
TOM: No.
(*Silence.*)
EVA: There was someone else, too.
TOM: What?
EVA: I saw someone else. Watching. Watching me. Have you seen anyone?
TOM: No.
EVA: Over the wall . . . beyond the rose beds.
TOM: Oh.
EVA: A woman.
TOM: Mrs Henniker.
EVA: But you said . . .
TOM: The woman next door. Her name is Mrs Henniker.
She's a widow.
She lives next door.
She's our neighbour. We have to have neighbours.
Don't look at me like that, Eva. She was trying to be friendly.
EVA: She was staring at me. In the end, I had to go back into the house, and shut the door.
TOM: She wanted a chance . . . an opening . . .
EVA: Why?
TOM: Perhaps she's lonely . . .
EVA: I can't help her.
TOM: Couldn't you try?
EVA: I don't like being stared at.
TOM: She seems a nice woman.
EVA: It's all beginning again, isn't it? She wants to find out.
TOM: No.

EVA: Even here, they know. You said there was no reason, no reason at all why anyone should know anything about us. About any of it . . . If we move right away, you said, no one need ever know. That's what you told me, Tom.

TOM: And that was true.

EVA: Then why was she staring at me like that over the wall?

TOM: She was simply trying to be . . . friendly . . . neighbourly. People *do*.

EVA: Then she will start asking questions, and then I shall have to lie, but that won't help, she'll still find out.

TOM: Why on earth should she?

EVA: And it will all begin, all over again.

TOM: Yes, if you let it.

EVA: What?

TOM: If that's what you want.

EVA: *Want?*

TOM: Yes. It is, isn't it?
You feed off it. I've watched you . . . I've been watching you for nearly two years, and during all that time, it hasn't lessened, it has grown . . . it's grown like a cancer . . . and now it's spread out inside you . . . it fills your mind . . . you can't think of anything else . . . it feeds you . . . and you feed it back . . . I think you would die, now, without it.
(*Silence*.)
I'm sorry.

EVA: It would have been better to change our name. I've always said that.

TOM: Spencer is a perfectly common name. There are thousands of people called Spencer.

EVA: 'Spencer son on murder charge.'

TOM: Eva . . .

EVA: 'Spencer girl raped before death, Post Mortem reveals.'

TOM: Don't, Eva.

EVA: 'Spencer boy found hanged.'

TOM: I said stop it. Shut up!
(*Silence*.)

EVA: Names and faces. People remember. They remember

for years. I can remember the names of all the people who were hanged for murder when I was a girl . . .

TOM: That is not the same thing, we've been over this . . .

EVA: Haig, Bentley, Christie, Ruth Ellis . . .
But he had to hang himself.
People remember, you see.

TOM: You remember.

EVA: Oh yes.

TOM: But I do not want to.

EVA: You've no choice, Tom.

TOM: Oh yes. I want to be free of it. I wanted to come here, to this place, to this house, where there are no memories, and which has nothing to do with the past for us . . . because I want to be myself again. I haven't been myself for more than two years, Eva.

EVA: 'A Spencer father.'

TOM: No!
I want to be myself. That's all. Here.

EVA: With me.

TOM: With you.

EVA: But it isn't possible, Tom. You know that. They're here with us aren't they?

TOM: No. Not with us. Just with you. You're the one who brought them.

EVA: I go in and out of those rooms upstairs, looking for them. I talk to them.

TOM: Don't do it. It's unnatural.

EVA: I want them.

TOM: You cannot have them, Eva. Can you? They're dead. They are both dead.
(*Silence.*)
Sometimes . . .

EVA: What?

TOM: No.

EVA: Yes. Sometimes . . . you said.

TOM: No.
(*Silence.*)
Very well then. Sometimes, I have thought of . . . going away.

EVA: On a holiday?

TOM: No. Not a holiday. But . . . going away. Beginning all over again.

EVA: We came here.

TOM: I mean . . . somewhere else . . . altogether. Another country.

EVA: I don't want to live in another country.

TOM: Not . . . you.

EVA: *Leave me?* Leave me here? Is that what you want to do?

TOM: I don't *want* to. I . . .

EVA: Go away by yourself.

TOM: You see . . . I think . . . sometimes . . . no, quite often . . . almost every day now . . . that I shall go mad. Because I don't know who I am. I lost the person I used to be and I feel I'm . . . no one. Not a person. Not any longer.

EVA: 'Spencer father.'

TOM: *No!* That's over.

EVA: It will never be over.

TOM: In another country no one would know about it. Me. My name.

EVA: A common name, you said.

TOM: You know what I'm saying . . . there would be no chance. It couldn't follow me there.

EVA: No, you would take it with you. It's part of you, now, you will carry it about with you until you die.

TOM: No!

EVA: You can't do anything about it. Nor can I. Why can't you accept that? I have.

TOM: Oh yes!

EVA: They were your children. Our children. The children we made.

TOM: Our children are dead.

EVA: We aren't.

TOM: But I feel as if I am dead. And I don't want that. Not any more. I want to be alive.

EVA: How strange.

TOM: No, it is not strange. It is normal and natural and human. The usual human desire.

EVA: Is it? Yes. I'd forgotten.

TOM: Yes.
EVA: I wonder what will happen?
TOM: What?
EVA: To me. When you go.
TOM: Eva . . .
EVA: Oh, you'll go. Of course. I see that now.
TOM: I don't know.
EVA: Yes. Yes, and you should, Tom. Get out, get away, that would be the right thing. There's hope for you, I see that too. You can be saved. Run, Tom, run.
(*Silence.*)
TOM: But there would be no need . . . even to think of it . . . if you would let me forget. That's all. I could stay here. I want to stay.
EVA: What you want is to forget.
TOM: Yes. To try.
EVA: But . . . then what?
TOM: This new beginning. A life for us both . . . here.
EVA: New house. New garden.
TOM: Yes!
EVA: A lot of tulips and an apple orchard with a few woolly sheep.
TOM: Good things. An ordinary, happy life. Is it wrong to want that? I don't see how it can be.
EVA: But it could never be happy, how can you say that? How can you ever imagine it?
TOM: We've talked like this before. We don't understand each other any better.
EVA: No.
TOM: Eva . . . things do . . . happen. Terrible things. All the time. Children die. There are . . . wars . . . massacres . . . bombs . . . dreadful accidents . . . there is . . . murder and rape and . . . and the violence in the world and there are silly, pointless mistakes that hurt people . . . but . . . there are survivors, too. What about them?
EVA: They . . . just survive.
TOM: No. They live. They have to.
EVA: No.
TOM: Do you remember that man . . . where was it? In

Wales, I think. Yes. His whole family . . . his mother and father, his sister, his wife and children . . . even their dog . . . were all kept prisoner by those . . . madmen, for a week, and then they were blown up . . . set fire to . . . everything gone . . . he was outside the house, talking to them, pleading with them and . . . they brought his family to the window . . . one by one, to show him . . . and then . . . they blew them up . . . do you remember that? Well . . . he survived. And in the end, he lived . . . he married again, they had a child . . . he . . .

EVA: Oh, *traitor*!

TOM: No, no! Why?

EVA: Christopher was right. He did the only thing.

TOM: Christopher ran away.

EVA: It was a brave thing to do, Tom.

TOM: To hang yourself, by a leather belt, from a nail in the wall of a cell? Bravery?

EVA: He knew there would be no 'new life'.

TOM: Christopher was sick.

EVA: He doesn't regret it. I've told you that before. I know it. He said so. It was the only thing to do and he did it. He isn't unhappy.

TOM: Stop that, you've left all that behind you, I won't listen to it. You promised you would never talk like that again.

EVA: In the new house, in the new life.

TOM: Yes.

EVA: But I still remember it all. It's made no difference.

TOM: Eva, what more can I try and do for you? What else can I give you?

EVA: Nothing. No, no. You've been very good. You're a good person, Tom. Never think I don't know it. You should run . . . go away, get out, take your chance. There's nothing here for you.

TOM: I'd find nothing anywhere else.

EVA: There was a woman I used to see sometimes . . . in a shop . . . the florist's shop, that was it, she worked there . . . and sometimes in the doctor's surgery . . . a big woman with coiled up hair . . . Her husband lay down on the railway line. Just got up, quite early one morning, and took her a cup of tea . . . and then went out . . . and lay down on the railway line . . . She didn't know why . . . she never had any idea why . . . she said there was no note, there was nothing wrong that she knew of . . . they'd been quite happy, she said . . . I used to talk to her, sometimes . . . And then, I saw her with a man . . . I mean, arm in arm with a man . . . I couldn't speak to her after that . . . couldn't look at her. I didn't understand her.

TOM: No.

EVA: She hadn't seemed hard . . . but she must have been mustn't she?

TOM: Why? Why, for God's sake?

EVA: And then I saw that she was only doing what people expected and what they wanted . . . because . . . they are so embarrassed.

TOM: People want . . . need . . . things to be normal.

EVA: 'Go to classes . . . something you can give yourself up to . . . you could paint . . . painting's supposed to be so therapeutic . . . or music . . . and then there are all those people who need you . . . who are so much worse off than you are . . . all those people to go and visit . . . the old and the mad and the lonely people . . . take them to tea . . . or out for a jaunt in the country, they do so appreciate it . . . or a dog? Why not get a dog, a dog's such good company . . . you get a lot of love, from a dog.

TOM: We could have a dog . . . here I mean a dog, though . . . not a bitch. Bitches ruin the lawn.

EVA: *I don't want a dog.*

TOM: People just want to help . . . they only try to think of something that will help you.

EVA: On the day of the inquest, I was making a cup of tea . . . and I turned on the wireless . . . it's something to do isn't it, a habit . . . fill the kettle, see what's on . . . Well, there was an Indian, telling a joke about vasectomy . . . I can't remember, something about a free transistor radio with every operation, or else a digital watch . . . or . . . and I laughed . . . well, I

suppose you were meant to . . . but . . . I mean, before I could stop myself, it caught me unawares and . . . *I laughed.* On that day. I stopped thinking about my son who murdered his sister and hanged himself and laughed.
(*She is sobbing.*)

TOM: I know. My darling, I *know*.

EVA: In the night, I wake up and I hear them . . . crying or calling out . . . I know it's them. And I get out of bed and start to go to them . . . All those days, Tom . . . days and years, and they've gone, they are nothing any more. All the things they ever said and did . . . I ever said to them . . . I'd have smothered them, you know, smothered them with their pillows when they were babies. If I could have seen the future. Just . . . murdered them quietly then.

TOM: No.

EVA: Will it ever end, Tom? Will it? Do I have to die first? And then what?

TOM: I don't know. Perhaps it will get better. Perhaps it has.

EVA: No. Oh, no.

TOM: Yes. Today . . . look, you were planting the bulbs . . . enjoying it, it made your back ache, you were talking about the bulbs we used to have . . . and an orchard and . . . oh, something anything but it was not *that*. At first, there was nothing, nothing at all . . . but then, gradually . . . for a minute or two or . . . if you let it happen. That isn't wrong.
It isn't too late, Eva. We're not even old.

EVA: No.

TOM: *Please.*
(*Silence.*)

EVA: Where would you go?

TOM: Nowhere.

EVA: Yes . . . tell me . . . you've thought about it, you must have . . .

TOM: I shan't go anywhere . . . You know that.

EVA: Well . . .
(*Silence.*)

TOM: It's too cold to sit here any longer.
EVA: Damp . . . yes, there's that damp smell.
TOM: Yes. Autumn.
EVA: The day has gone.
TOM: Yes. I'll pick up these bulbs for you. Put them in the shed.
EVA: Tom . . .
TOM: Yes?
EVA: You won't go.
TOM: No.
EVA: There is nothing else, you see. I have . . . nothing at all.
TOM: I know.
EVA: I wouldn't want to be left alone . . . with them.
TOM: No.
EVA: There is . . . only you.
TOM: I'm here.
EVA: (*Getting up.*) Oh . . . my back really aches.
TOM: A hot bath . . . and I'll make you some more tea . . . bring it up to you.
EVA: Yes. Thank you.
TOM: Just let me clear these up.
EVA: (*Going a few paces off.*) Over there? Don't you think? On that side? The orchard?
TOM: Yes . . .
EVA: I shall need to pace it out properly . . . you have to have the right distance between the trees, or you cramp the roots . . . and old apples . . . the sort no one grows any more . . . Orleans Reinette . . . Lord Lambourn . . . James Grieve . . . that sort . . .
TOM: Yes.
EVA: But you're right . . . I'll go in and have a hot bath now.
TOM: Right.
EVA: (*A bit further off.*) Are you coming in?
TOM: I told you . . . I'll clear up these things . . .
EVA: Right. (*Going*)
(*Pause. Door closes to house.*)
TOM: Then, I can be here . . . with them. Just them. No one else. No one . . . if I stay out here by myself . . . they'll

come. Perhaps they will come to me too . . . I'll look round and I'll see them.
I just . . . want to see them.

THE END

WINTER

A Play for Radio

First Broadcast in 1985

The setting is the sun lounge of the Home. It is November. There is perhaps a slight echo in the place, as no one else is there and there is no carpet on the floor, and the windows and roof are glassed in. The chairs are the sort of wicker basket chairs that creak both when being sat in and got up from, and from time to time during the conversation, at a slight shift or movement.

MAY *has been sitting for a few moments. She has begun to knit.* FRANK *walks in slowly. Settles down next to her. After a moment . . .*

MAY: Oh? There you are. Did you . . . ?

FRANK: No, no.
No.

MAY: You didn't?

FRANK: Clammed up straight away.

MAY: Nothing?

FRANK: Not a dickie.
(*Silence. She sighs.*)

MAY: Oh dear.
But what exactly did you . . . ?

FRANK: Say? I asked. Outright. Told her. 'Mrs Bromidge and I are a bit concerned about Edna,' is what I said.

MAY: How she is.

FRANK: How she is. It is four days, after all. I mean to say . . .

MAY: We are her friends.

FRANK: 'It was Sunday night' I said, 'and it is now Thursday. And no one has said a word. Not a dickie. Not allowed to go up there, doors kept shut and all you get out of Sister Hamilton you could write on a postage stamp.

MAY: Did you see Sister Hamilton?

FRANK: I did not.

MAY: Oh dear.

FRANK: The plain fact of the matter is, to put it bluntly, I told her, that we want to know exactly what is wrong with her. What the doctor said. What the outlook is. Why she can't have visitors. (*Raised voice.*) What are you keeping from us?

MAY: Oh dear.

FRANK: Her eyes are like bullfrogs. They don't only protrude. They glisten.

MAY: But what exactly did she . . .

FRANK: Minces up her mouth. Can hardly get half a dozen words out of the corner. Like passing prune stones. 'Miss Turk is not at all well. I'm afraid she really could not cope with any visitors just at present. Doctor has said so.'
Well, when will she, dammit? This is a free country and we're not in prison, you know. Though mind you . . .

MAY: I don't think it's right. I really don't. She might be – well – distressed. She might want to say something she couldn't say to . . . one of them. Only to one of us.

FRANK: I know it.

MAY: I don't like to think of her. Ill. Up there. Without any of us. I wonder if anyone else has tried?

FRANK: Mrs Dabbs has tried. Major Pritchett has enquired. Gobbed off.
(*May sighs. Knits on.*)

MAY: It's very strange without her.

FRANK: Damn funny.

MAY: Quiet.

FRANK: You're so used to it. Head of the table. Best armchair up to the t.v.

MAY: Empty.

FRANK: Damn funny.

MAY: When I first came here, you know, I didn't care for her at all. I found her . . . vulgar.

FRANK: Loud.

MAY: Common, even. Even . . .
FRANK: Coarse.
MAY: Well . . . yes.
FRANK: Puts the life into this place though doesn't she? Well, doesn't she?
MAY: Life, yes. She's always . . . lively.
FRANK: I said, if it's some sort of infection . . .
MAY: Oh, I don't think it could be that, I'm sure we'd have been told. Besides, nobody else has . . .
FRANK: No. No. But I wanted to give her a lead.
MAY: But?
FRANK: Not a dickie. Shut up like a clam. 'Miss Turk's illness is hers alone, Mr Gobday. I can set your mind at rest on that score.' Quite nasty. Silly old fart.
MAY: Now!
FRANK: She is.
MAY: I think it could be her heart.
FRANK: Stroke.
MAY: Perhaps she's become paralysed. Perhaps she can't speak. People sometimes can't, after strokes. Perhaps she wants to see one of us and *isn't able to say so.*
FRANK: Anything could be happening. You're powerless.
MAY: I thought at supper . . . how quiet it seemed. I began to notice things I'd forgotten about.
FRANK: Mr Shingler's false teeth.
(*He makes a click-suck noise.*)
MAY: Oh yes. Oh, don't.
She makes all that sort of thing so . . .
FRANK: Her laughing. That's what I kept hearing. Her laughing. Hoot-hoot-hoot.
MAY: When I first came here, I found that irritating. But . . .
FRANK: Life and soul.
MAY: Yes.
Oh dear.
If I felt it was all for the best. If I could be quite *sure.* For her own good. Well naturally we only want what would be the best for Edna.
FRANK: You need to be sure.
MAY: It's just that . . . we *know* her.
FRANK: Sitting in that chair.

MAY: Head of the table.
FRANK: Cock of the walk.
MAY: Queen Bee.
(*Silence.*)
I didn't tell you. Last night.
FRANK: Last night?
MAY: Oh dear.
FRANK: What's this about?
MAY: (*Blows her nose.*)
You see, I woke up. Something woke me. I don't as a rule. Well, not unless I need to . . . Well. It was three o'clock. I looked at my alarum, straight away. Just on three. And then, of course, I couldn't go back. I got up. I had to get up then. There were footsteps. I knew it. I'd heard footsteps.
I went and stood by my door. And then I opened it. I went and stood on the landing. Her door must have been ajar. Just a shade. I could see a light.
I could hear her. I could hear her breathing. It was dreadful, Frank. Like a child with croup. My son had croup once. At Herne Bay. I could hear her, fighting to get her breath. And voices. Murmurs. I couldn't make out what.
I stood there, listening. I didn't like to go to . . . well, in case somone heard me. In the end, just closed my door and went back to bed. I didn't sleep. Not for a long time. I heard them go. The footsteps. I don't know what time it was then. After that, I just lay awake, thinking about Edna, and remembering her breathing. And I thought, well, this is how it'll be. Sometime or other. For Edna. For you. For me. All of us. I thought, that's what we're here for, isn't it, that's why we've come.
(*She begins to weep quietly.*)
I thought I'd have liked someone there with me then. A hand. Or . . . Someone. You say you're all right, here you're never alone, there's always someone you can ring for. But when it comes to it, you don't, do you? You just don't bring yourself to do it.
(*Silence.*)
(*May blows her nose. Cries a little more. Then stops. Shifts a*

bit in her chair. Resumes knitting.)

FRANK: You could go up. Nothing to stop you. What's to stop you? Just . . . go up.

MAY: Oh, no. No.

FRANK: Why not? Tell me why not? *I* couldn't. Well, of course not. Not my place. But you could go up to her.

MAY: Just walk in?

FRANK: Just walk in.

MAY: I wouldn't like to set her back. I wouldn't want to upset her. Get her into trouble.

FRANK: You'd see then.

MAY: Yes. I would see.

FRANK: If you want to.

(*Silence.*)

MAY: I got a shock today. I was looking in the window of Forbes and Haverlow. At the wedding dresses. Nasty cheap things, all nylon. And I caught sight of myself.

FRANK: Reflection.

MAY: In the window. Yes.

I saw myself. I don't like the way that new girl had cut my hair. It makes me look older. It's like a pudding basin. At the back. I could see it under my hat. Like they cut people's hair in institutions. In hospitals. And places. Is that what I look like?

FRANK: This is an institution.

MAY: What would *she* say?

FRANK: 'Don't let them get to you, my ducky.'

MAY: 'Are you a-hearing me?'

FRANK: 'Up the fogies!'

(*They both laugh. Then stop dead.*)

MAY: I never knew how much to believe her. About the music halls. And that second husband. About the variety act.

FRANK: 'Knew,' you said. 'Knew.'

MAY: I said?

FRANK: You said 'I never knew.'

(*Silence.*)

FRANK: I thought of bringing up the subject of the heater again. Pick my moment.

MAY: A heater in here?

FRANK: It is November.
MAY: They just don't expect anyone to use it.
FRANK: No law against us using it.
MAY: In winter. Well . . . people don't . . . use a sun lounge, in winter.
FRANK: We do.
MAY: You can't ask for special treatment.
FRANK: Who can't?
MAY: You can bring a rug down. It's nice and quiet though. Looking through the window. In the daytime. I like that tree. I've always liked that.
FRANK: A gale or two, and that'll be that. Till the spring.
MAY: It was one of the first things. When I came here. I thought, if I can sit and look at that tree in the garden, perhaps things won't be too bad. And the grass.
FRANK: Should I start something up? About a heater? We're fully entitled.
MAY: Oh, don't make a fuss. I hate causing a fuss. We're all right, aren't we? No one bothers.
FRANK: I bother. I get cold.
MAY: You know what I mean. Unless you'd rather be in there.
FRANK: With the rest of them.
MAY: Yes.
FRANK: Mr Shingler's false teeth. Granny Bunce, snorting.
MAY: Shh.
FRANK: They can't hear us.
MAY: But don't like it, that's all. It's . . .
FRANK: What?
MAY: 'May with the pudding haircut.'
FRANK: 'Frank with his bad feet.'
MAY: It's easy to laugh.
FRANK: Yes. Easy to laugh. (*Neither laughs.*)
(*Silence.*)
FRANK: It raises an interesting question, of course. Her dying.
MAY: *Dying?*
FRANK: There's always that possibility. In here. Always on the cards.
MAY: Edna isn't *dying*.

FRANK: How do you know? You don't.
MAY: You stop that, do you hear? Stop it. I won't listen. I'm not listening to talk like that.
FRANK: Dying.
MAY: *Stop it!* I'm going back. I'm not sitting here.
FRANK: Granny Bunce will be watching the snooker. Major Plackett will want that variety show. Whose side will you go in on?
MAY: You're a hurtful old man.
FRANK: The question is, who'll take over?
MAY: What?
FRANK: You said you weren't listening.
MAY: It's too cold to sit out here. Look at me, my fingers are white, I can hardly hold the wool. It's ridiculous. This is a *sun-lounge*.
FRANK: Her armchair. Place at the head of the table. It's hers now, but if she were to go? No one sitting there at the moment, of course . . . too respectful. Besides, you don't want to tempt fate. She isn't dead yet.
MAY: You stop that! I said stop it!
FRANK: There's a question of succession.
MAY: That's a wicked thing to say!
FRANK: Ha!
(*Silence.*)
I thought you were off.
MAY: I think – somedays – I say to myself . . . I'll run away. Go. I could. What's to stop me? I'll walk out of that front door and down that path and never come back. Never, run away.
FRANK: Oh yes.
MAY: I could go to Deirdre's. Deirdre would have me.
FRANK: Oh yes.
MAY: I said I never would. I wouldn't put on her. I've seen too much of that.
FRANK: Being a burden.
MAY: I wish Deirdre had married.
FRANK: And then again, there's Australia.
MAY: I was invited. I've got enough put by, you know. For the fare. I could go.
FRANK: Oh yes.

MAY: I've never met his wife. We've spoken on the telephone, of course.

FRANK: At Christmas.

MAY: And to the grand-children.

FRANK: Shrinks the world.

MAY: There's no one to make me stop here.

FRANK: No.

MAY: No.
Oh dear.
(*Silence. She has settled back again.*)

FRANK: Wait a day. Then I'll ask. I'll tackle her.

MAY: About Edna?

FRANK: About that heater.

MAY: They watch us, you know.

FRANK: Oh yes.

MAY: I've seen them.

FRANK: Tongues clacking.

MAY: Well, they could come and sit out here. If they chose. Anyone could.

FRANK: What's to stop them?

MAY: I suppose . . .

FRANK: What?

MAY: Nothing.

FRANK: You were thinking.

MAY: No. I wish I hadn't thought it. I don't know why it came into my mind. It was you, starting on . . . about her chair and her place at the table. It wouldn't have come into my mind if it hadn't been for that.

FRANK: Go on then.

MAY: Stop it!
(*Silence.*)
It isn't as if she's much older . . . well . . . a couple of years . . .

FRANK: So she says!

MAY: What do you mean by that?

FRANK: That kind of woman . . . her background . . . knock a good few years off. Probably always has. Well, of course she would. Becomes a habit.

MAY: Oh no!

FRANK: Well, why ever not, why ever not? Bit of vanity.

Where's the harm?
MAY: You're seventy-six.
FRANK: It's different for a man.
MAY: I'm seventy-five.
FRANK: That's different.
MAY: Seventy-seven, she says.
FRANK: She says.
MAY: Oh dear.
FRANK: Eighty, if you ask me.
MAY: She never does have a birthday.
FRANK: Exactly. There you are then.
MAY: But she'd want a birthday. If she'd been eighty. They make a nice fuss of you when you're eighty.
FRANK: Or ninety, or a hundred.
MAY: They give you a party.
FRANK: Or dead.
MAY: You stop that.
FRANK: They give you a party. After the funeral. Ham and tongue and an iced cake.
MAY: That's not the same thing.
FRANK: No. You're not there to eat it.
MAY: Stop that.
FRANK: You have to face facts?
MAY: No you don't.
FRANK: Ha!
(*Silence.*)
MAY: If you want to know, it was her room. There now, it's out. I've said it.
I wish I hadn't said it.
FRANK: It's a very nice room. Onto the garden.
MAY: That little balcony.
FRANK: Bit bigger all round.
MAY: It's the best room in the house.
FRANK: Oh yes.
MAY: Not that I'm envious.
FRANK: Only wondering.
MAY: Yes.
No!
FRANK: Why don't you ask?
MAY: I wish I'd never said it. May God forgive me, I didn't

mean to say it!

FRANK: Well she can't hear you.

MAY: It's not right.

FRANK: She's not dead yet.

MAY: I'm a wicked old woman. (*Weeping.*)

FRANK: How would it be if I was to go? Take the law into my own hands. Why not? How would that be?

MAY: They'd hear you.

FRANK: Let them.

MAY: They can make your life . . . very unpleasant. You know that. Little things.

FRANK: Let them.

MAY: Sister Hamilton can be so . . . sharp. I've prayed, sometimes . . . if I'm taken ill . . . when it happens . . . if it happens . . . if I have to ring that bell . . . Please don't let it be Sister Hamilton.

FRANK: Her night off.

MAY: Oh yes.

FRANK: I'm not afraid of Sister Hamilton.

MAY: Poor Edna.

FRANK: I'd just get up from here and go. Through the hall. Up the stairs. Onto the landing. Along the corridor.

MAY: Knock.

FRANK: Open the door and walk in.

MAY: You'd see for yourself, then.

FRANK: Ask them, they'll never let on. Ask till you're blue in the face. Treated like children. 'Please, Matron.' (*Shouts*) *I'm a grown man of 76, do you hear?*

MAY: Oh dear.

FRANK: Cheer the old girl up.

MAY: You don't know what you'd find.

FRANK: Might be nothing. Nothing at all. Bit of a chill.

MAY: But if it was just a bit of a chill, why wouldn't they have said? Why would they want to keep her shut upstairs away from us and not let anyone in? Why would they want to be so secretive about it all?

FRANK: Power. They're power mad.

MAY: We pay to live here, you know. This is a guest home. This isn't a prison. We pay.

FRANK: Little Hitlers. Women like Sister Hamilton.

MAY: I don't think anyone would believe . . . how sharp she can be.

FRANK: Of course, when she's well, when she's on form, she makes mincemeat of the lot of them. Mincemeat. They daren't say Boo. *And* Sister Hamilton.

MAY: The things she's said sometimes! Behind their backs. Oh, I've said, Shhh Edna! She isn't out of the room hardly, she hasn't closed the door. She'll *hear* you!

FRANK: And who's she, Lady Muck? Let her hear. Constipated old . . .

MAY: Shhhh!

FRANK: I can tell you what she could do with!

MAY: When I first came here, I used to . . . well, blush. Sometimes. I thought she was just a bit . . . coarse.

FRANK: Fruity.

MAY: Not quite . . .

FRANK: A lady.

MAY: Till I got to know her.

FRANK: Heart of gold.

MAY: Oh yes.

FRANK: Doesn't care a brass farthing.

MAY: Then I came to admire her.

FRANK: Got spirit.

MAY: Oh, yes.

FRANK: She liked an audience.

MAY: Well, of course she would . . . her background.

FRANK: Oh yes.

MAY: I wonder how she's managing without one.

FRANK: Up there.

MAY: Just Sister Hamilton.

FRANK: And Her.

MAY: The doctor never has time to stop long.

FRANK: In and out.

MAY: If I close my eyes, I can hear it now. I can hear it, as clearly as if I was still standing there. That breathing. Her . . . struggling for her breath.

FRANK: You want to keep your ears open from now on. Footsteps.

MAY: Oh, I shan't sleep now.

FRANK: I remember when old Fred Cartwright went. That

was in the middle of the night. Footsteps . . . bumping up . . . bumping down. Just saw the tail end of the stretcher, going down the stair well . . . face covered in a blanket . . . They like to slip them away.
You want to keep your ears open.

MAY: Oh, Edna.

FRANK: Well, what can you do? There's nothing you can do.

MAY: They can't lock her in. Can they?

FRANK: Wouldn't put it past them.

MAY: But the fire risk? They make all that fuss about not locking your door, because of the fire risk.

FRANK: Well, it's one law for us and . . .

MAY: She hasn't done anything wrong has she? This isn't a prison. What has Edna ever done to anyone, you tell me that?

FRANK: They don't listen.

MAY: She kept me going.

FRANK: Her cheek!

MAY: Made up like that, eye-shadow and rouge and perfume, by ten o'clock every morning. She wouldn't let them cut her hair like a pudding basin. I used to look at Edna, if I felt a bit down, and she kept me going.

FRANK: 'Kept' you said, 'She kept me going.'

MAY: Oh stop that, stop it.

FRANK: She'd no family.

MAY: None left.

FRANK: 'Never were much to me, my ducky. You're better off on your tod.'

MAY: I talked to her about Deirdre sometimes. I worry. That Deirdre never married. But Edna cheered me up. 'Men' she said, 'I know all about men. All right for the night.' Oh dear? 'Tell your Deirdre, she's better off.' Only of course I never could have talked to her about it. Deirdre. I wouldn't know how to . . . raise the subject. She can be quite . . . sharp.

FRANK: The nights are drawing in.

MAY: I don't like the dark evenings. I like to look out onto the garden.

FRANK: Another winter.

MAY: I wonder if she's been able to look out of her window

. . . onto the garden.

FRANK: She's got the best view.

MAY: Yes.

FRANK: And then Christmas.

MAY: Oh, I like Christmas.

FRANK: Won't be the same. Without Edna.

MAY: Stop that. You stop it. I won't have you talk like that.

FRANK: Got to face facts.

MAY: You don't *know*.

FRANK: No.

MAY: None of us does. They're the only ones who know.

FRANK: Oh yes.

MAY: The only way you can find out, is to go.

FRANK: Yes.

MAY: Just go up there. Walk across the hall . . .

FRANK: . . . Up the stairs . . .

MAY: . . . Onto the landing . . .

FRANK: . . . Along the corridor . . .

MAY: . . . To her door.

FRANK: Knock.

MAY: And go in. Just . . . go in.

FRANK: Oh yes.

MAY: That's the only way you'll ever get to the bottom of it.

FRANK: Get at the truth. Oh yes.

MAY: That's the only way.

FRANK: You're quite right.

MAY: Oh dear.

(*Silence.*)

FRANK: But I will ask. Pick my moment. Get her in the proper mood. You have to be careful. Size things up and then . . . jump in. Then I'll ask.

MAY: About Edna?

FRANK: About that heater.

(*She sighs. Chairs creak. She knits on.*)

THE END

HERE COMES THE BRIDE

A Play for Radio

First Broadcast in 1980

(*Sound of milk float drawing up. Milk bottles chinking. Milkman walks up path whistling Mendelssohn's 'Wedding March'. Sets bottles on step. Knocks on front door. Door opens.*)

MILKMAN: (*Sings snatch of 'Wedding March'*) Good morning, good morning, good morning. Three pints and a half of cream.

(LOUISA *yawns loudly in acknowledgement.*)

Well, where is she then? Where's the blushing bride?

LOUISA: It's half-past *six*!

MILKMAN: Day's half over. Ah well, sorry to have missed her, got to press on. You tell her for me then, 'All the best from Len', OK?

LOUISA: OK.

(MILKMAN *goes off, whistling again. Door closes on* LOUISA*'s next yawn.*)

(*Bedroom.*)

GRACE: *Waking*) Still not sure it's right . . .

EDWIN: Huh? (*groans*).

GRACE: Too bright. Gaudy. Well isn't it? Marjorie's wearing grey.

EDWIN: It's not a funeral.

GRACE: Cup of tea?

EDWIN: I'll go.

GRACE: No, no. (*Gets up*) Thought I'd never sleep.

EDWIN: I'm the one in the grey. Look at it. Fancy dress!

GRACE: I haven't heard a sound from her room.

EDWIN: (*the Mendelssohn*) Pom-pom-po-pom-pom-pom –. . .
(*Staircase.*)
GRACE: Oh, Louisa . . .
LOUISA: Me. (*Yawns*)
GRACE: She's still asleep.
LOUISA: Fancy.
GRACE: Now you'll tell me what you really think. But taking another look at it in the morning light, I am a bit worried.
LOUISA: Ma, your outfit is not too bright, it is not gaudy, you are not going to steal the limelight, you will not be mutton dressed as lamb. OK? It's too boring.
(*Bathroom door slams. Taps turned on within.*)
(*Front door.* POSTMAN*'s footsteps.* POSTMAN *whistling 'This is my Lovely Day'. Knocks. Door opens.*)
POSTMAN: Four greetings telegrams, pile of cards. Lovely day for it, you've picked.
GRACE: Happy the bride . . .
POSTMAN: . . . the sun shines on. Rained cats and dogs on mine.
GRACE: And mine! Oh, dear.
POSTMAN: Never a cross word from that day to this, all the same. Give her a kiss from Postie, eh?
(*Goes away humming 'This is my Lovely Day'. Door closes.*)
GRACE: Now she ought to have breakfast, but of course she won't. Nobody will. I couldn't, I know that. And a dozen things still to do. (*Calling*) Louisa! Are you out of the bathroom?
(*Bathroom. Sound of water sloshing.*)
LOUISA: (*Cheerfully*) Bloody wedding!
(*Bedroom.*)
HELENA: Like a lot of mice scurrying about behind the walls. I hear you. I know you. But they've enjoyed themselves so much. Well, Mother has. I couldn't have taken it away from her could I? Eldest daughter, first wedding, everything happy ever after. Isn't it?
(*Gets out of bed, goes over to window. Draws curtains. Birdsong from garden.*)
And I slept so well. Shouldn't have done, I suppose. Hungry, too. That can't be right. Oh, the sunshine!

Look! Dew on the grass. The old swing in the apple tree.
(*Creak of swing.*)

HELENA AS CHILD: Higher. Higher. Up in the sky to heaven. I'm going up to heaven!

HELENA: *So* happy. Never so happy again. I should be sad just now. This room, this house . . . all of my life. Twenty-six years. And nothing's changed. Doesn't seem like it, anyway. The orchard where I hid among the branches. Found the hedgehog, slept out all night in a tent. The broken brick wall behind the lilacs. He kept saying, I'll see to that, next fine weekend. And over the hedges and fences and bushes, the lawn and trees and flowerbeds and sheds of all the houses down the avenue. And never again. I should cry. Feel . . . Feel nothing. Neither sad nor glad. Numb. Don't think of it.
(*Knock on door.*)

HELENA: Hello?

LOUISA: Tea. I thought you'd rather have me.

HELENA: Hi.

LOUISA: Hi yourself.
(HELENA *drinks with pleasure.*)
Oh, three messages, Len, the milkman, Bob, the postman, love and kisses, you know.

HELENA: Thanks.

LOUISA: Feel good?

HELENA: Peculiar.

LOUISA: She's going on about the turquoise blue again.
(HELENA *groans.*)
That dress!

HELENA: There it is.

LOUISA: (*Touching the wedding dress. It rustles.*) The whole bit!

HELENA: Long and white. Yes.

LOUISA: The whole bit.
(*Going to the door.*)
My God, you're cool . . .
(*Door closes.*)

HELENA: Cool. Yes. Ice. What's wrong? What is happening to me?
(*Delivery van draws up at front door. Footsteps. Door bell. Door opens.*)

DELIVERY MAN: Flowers for the Anderson wedding? One bouquet, two sprays, one button hole? Sign here please.

(*Sound of motorbike. Doorbell rings. Door opens.*)

TELEGRAM BOY: Greetings telegram, name of Anderson?

(*Interior.*)

EDWIN: (*Singing*) 'There was I, waiting at the church . . . a-waiting at the church . . .'.

GRACE: Edwin!

EDWIN: Sorry!

(*Bedroom. Knock on door.*)

HELENA: Come in, come in! Why's everybody so polite all of a sudden?

GRACE: (*Coming in*) Now Daddy has scraped the bottom of your shoes with the side of a matchbox . . .

HELENA: He's *what*?

GRACE: So you don't slip!

HELENA: Good heavens!

GRACE: What time's Bettina coming to do your hair?

HELENA: Ten.

GRACE: Ten. Right. Oh, dear. Now just you relax, darling. Everything's under control, don't worry about anything at all.

(*Door shuts.*)

HELENA: Not a thing. Except, who am I? What am I doing? Marrying a man whose face I cannot call to mind. Cannot. And somehow can't even make it matter.

(*Bedroom.*)

EDWIN: Look like a dog's dinner.

GRACE: Very handsome. But it's far too early, Edwin, you'll crease everything.

EDWIN: Thought I'd get out of the way, actually.

GRACE: (*To herself*) Ring the caterers, check about the missing tier. Did I tell you there was a missing tier?

LOUISA: (*Coming in*) Tears? Oh, God!

GRACE: *Cake* tier!

(*Bedroom.*)

HELENA: Cake, flowers, caterers, hymns, dresses, cars, shoes, hair, photographer, seating plans, champagne, plane tickets . . . up, up and away. It's like being on an express

train. Can't get off. They won't let you get off. Do I want to get off?
(*Door knocks.*)

EDWIN: Er . . . just wanted to . . .

HELENA: I say! Can I marry you?

EDWIN: Matter of fact, just glanced in the mirror by chance . . . quite impressed myself.

HELENA: 'Only don't tell your mother'.
(*Both laugh.*)

EDWIN: We've had some good times.

HELENA: Oh, Dad, Dad!

EDWIN: Sorry. (*Goes to window*) Always a nice room, this. The old swing.

HELENA: (*Brightly*) End of the road.

EDWIN: Of course, there's still Louisa.

HELENA: Never thought I'd be the first. She was the one. Louisa. When she was twelve, do you remember? Paul Potts!

EDWIN: Your mother cried all night. But you . . . no. Boys? You wanted to *be* a boy.

HELENA: Louisa wore the velvet party frocks.

EDWIN: Then Stephen. Just like that.

HELENA: Just like . . .

EDWIN: Well . . .

HELENA: All dressed up and nowhere to go? It's so early.

EDWIN: Thought I might stroll over and have a . . .

HELENA: . . . word with Henry! Keep a low profile.

EDWIN: You'll be all right, love. Yes. Not a care in the world. I'm more than content, anyway.

HELENA: See you later.
(*Door closes.*)
They all are. And it's really not surprising, is it? Stephen. When I first brought him home for a drink, that Sunday evening . . . paper patterns and material all over the floor . . . Dad in his shirtsleeves . . . might have been shot, any other time.

GRACE: (*Flashback*) 'I don't mind who you bring home, Helena, you know that, only I do like to have a bit of warning, get things straight. I might be in my dressing gown, anything . . .'

HELENA: But what happened?
HELENA: (*Flashback*) This is Stephen Rhodes.
GRACE: Well! Well, how very nice, Stephen. How do you do? Oh, sit down, dear, make yourself at home. If you won't mind just stepping *round* . . . there. Do excuse us, Stephen. I'll make a cup of coffee, given a moment.
EDWIN: Something a bit stronger, Stephen? Good to meet you. A beer? Drop of scotch to keep out the cold?
HELENA: That was that. Feet under the table and never looked back. Everybody's dream. Oh, and he is, he is. Yes. Only . . . suddenly, there are no horizons any more. I used to swing and swing, up up to heaven, I could do anything, anything might happen, anything at all. This way or that, what shall I choose, which shall it be? Years ahead, unrolling like a ribbon. Then . . . the absolutely certain. Security. I chose. I choose. Today. Does everything else stop, then? It's very quiet. Birds in the trees. The old swing. I am me. I am here and now. There is this. Only this.
There's still Louisa.
(*Bedroom.*)
LOUISA: (*Singing*) 'I went to her wedding, although I was dreading . . .' Aaah, blast! My God, I've gone blind . . . damn mascara . . . hell's teeth . . . Ma, I've gone blind . . . Oh, no, hang on, ok . . . 'You tripped down the aisle . . .' (*giggles*) Take my hat off to you, old girl. Landing one like that. Real Plum, is our Steve. Maybe I'll go to New York.
(*Bedroom.*)
HELENA: Tell the truth. She's clever, she's pretty, she's funny, she's got it all. I used to be sick with envy of my sister. Fairy Godmothers at her christening and she got the lot. And she's never known what to do with any of it. Still doesn't know. Tries this, has a go at that, strings of men, strings of jobs. Go, go, go, living on her nerves. I couldn't. No. This is me. All settled and peaceful now. Stephen. Mrs Stephen Rhodes. With this ring, I thee wed. Oh, God, it makes me shiver.
(*Knock on door.*)
GRACE: Betty's here, darling . . . and you still haven't had

your bath. What on earth are you thinking of?

HELENA: You went to church in the sidecar of a motorbike!

GRACE: Yes dear, but it was still wartime, now do hurry up. (*Door slams.*)

HELENA: It's like the tide coming in. And it washes over you. And you drown. But they've been all right haven't they? Wartime or not.

GRACE: (*Calling from below*)Helena! Helena!

HELENA: (*Opening door*) Coming.

GRACE: Telephone, Helena.

HELENA: Well, who on earth is it?

GRACE: Stephen.

HELENA: Stephen? Which Stephen?

LOUISA: (*Shrieks of laughter*) Which Stephen? My God, now I have heard everything!

(*Bedroom.*)

HELENA: If I turn round now, I shall be able to see myself. I daren't see myself. Look out of the window then. I can't bear it. Oh, come on. Look *now*.

(*Dress rustles as she turns.*)

(*whispers*) Who is it?

(*Door opens.*)

LOUISA: Car's here. I'm off. (*Pause*) You look incredible.

HELENA: I know.

LOUISA: Pa's having a gin. See you.

HELENA: Yes. Hey . . . you don't look bad yourself.

LOUISA: But then, I never do.

(*Laughs. Door slams.*)

HELENA: It's happening. It's nearly over.

EDWIN: (*Coming in*) Nearly ready? My!

HELENA: OK?

EDWIN: Very. Very OK my dear girl. (*Pause. He coughs*) Ah . . . think I can hear the car.

HELENA: Oh . . .

EDWIN: Take your time. All the time in the world. (*Goes out*)

HELENA: All – the – time – in – the – world. Oh God, I want to run away. It isn't me, it's someone else and I want to stay here. The birds in the garden. The old swing. What I was. And all those chances. My heart's going to jump out of my body.

EDWIN: (*Calling*) Helena? Helena . . . we're waiting for you.
HELENA: I can't go. I cannot move. *Oh, what will happen to me?*

(*Sound of 'Here comes the Bride'. Fades up, played softly on the church organ. Rustle, as the congregation rises. The music swells.*)

THE END

The World of Books

The Daily Telegraph 1977–1985

H. M. Tomlinson

In 1919, Katherine Mansfield wrote of him: 'He is alive; real things stir him profoundly. He has no need to exaggerate or heighten his effects. There is a quality in the prose that one might wish to call "magic": it is full of the quivering light and rainbow colours of the unsubstantial shore'.

To Rebecca West, in the following decade, he was 'a hesitant little man on whose shoulder perched all the strangeness of the steamy parts of the earth in the likeness of a multicoloured parrot. One of those supremely gifted writers who do it all by writing'. And Frank Swinnerton discerned that he had 'an eye and a sensitiveness rare among professional writers'.

He was also, from the publication of his first, and possibly best, book in 1912, until the last, shortly before his death in 1958, an immensely popular author. His name was H. M. Tomlinson, and I suspect that those who are familiar with it are now markedly fewer, while scarcely any of my own generation will have heard of him at all. That is a pity. He is a writer ripe for rediscovery.

Which is not to say that the whole body of his work – some twenty-six volumes – can now be undiscriminatingly admired. Much of it is simply dated. He wrote some fine essays, in the early years of the last war, a dozen of which are collected together in *The Wind is Rising*. They are partly evocations of a vanishing world, and especially of that old London in which he was born and reared, of docks and shipping offices and City warehouses, and they are not merely pretty nostalgia.

Tomlinson was passionately articulate in his defence of the civilised values and the absolute rights of the individual, and his rage in the face of the Nazi threat was inspiring. Nor was it simply flag-waving. He hated and condemned war, most clearly in a book called *Mars his Idol*, which arose out of personal experience – he was a war correspondent in Flanders in 1914 – and deep thought, and is both a reasoned and intensely felt tirade against what seemed to him the ultimate manifestation of human folly – battle. But the immediacy of it has cooled, and his war essays were of and for their own time.

Nor was he really a master of the art of fiction, although in one remarkable novel, *Gallions Reach*, is crystallised the very essence of Tomlinson's powerful mind and imagination. *All our Yesterdays* and *The Snows of Helicon* may be the titles of his which are best remembered, and certainly one can often find them in second-hand bookshops. But there is an uneasiness, a deadness even, about his fiction. He could not create convincing characters, nor lend artistic shape and credibility to a plot. He was a poet, philosopher, journalist, traveller, essayist, 'a topographer of the human spirit'. His novels are unlikely to enjoy any great revival.

Similarly, his two short works of literary criticism, though full of pertinent observations, are discursive and diffuse, giving us greater insight into the thoughts and work of H. M. Tomlinson than into those of their subjects, Thomas Hardy, whose friend and lifelong supporter he was, and Norman Douglas (though there is a great charm in the very incongruity of his appreciation of that unlikely fellow spirit).

What is left? And, indeed, is it proper to carve up an author in this way, retaining only a few items for wholehearted recommendation? For, particularly in Tomlinson's case, it is the whole man and his work we should get to know. He was so diverse, his experiences were so many in the course of a long life; he was versatile in the way men of letters are no longer, a 19th-century man of huge scope.

He was apprenticed in a shipping office at thirteen, reporter and adventurer by sea in his youth, and he developed a fine sense of perspective on man in his relation to the wide world. He was an acutely sensitive barometer of change, too, and he saw more than most of that in his lifetime – all epitomised for him by the change in ships from sail to steam.

He sounds a tough, physical man; in fact he was inward-looking, reflective, a little sombre.

But one had rather people read one or two books than nothing at all and perhaps signposts to his best work are useful. The quintessential Tomlinson is to be found in *The Sea and the Jungle*, which is a great travel book, ultimately concerned with the spiritual, as well as the physical journeying of man, with how he faces, endures and is developed by loneliness, danger, fear and the sights of a strange new world. It is the record of Tomlinson's own voyage to Brazil and up the Amazon and Madeira rivers in the first English steamer to make that passage; the descriptive writing is unforgettable and very disturbing.

All his finest and most characteristic writing is of the sea, and none of it is in print, but *The Turn of the Tide*, *Under the Red Ensign*, and *Gallions Reach* are all obtainable, with a little trouble, and endlessly rewarding.

He will never again be truly fashionable because many will be put off by the discursive, leisurely, ruminating style, and because his conspicuous virtues are not contemporary ones. But so much of what he has to say cuts as sharply as ever, his vision is so clear. He is, most precious of all, the opener of magic casements.

(1977)

Cider with Rosie

by Laurie Lee

Look along the shelves of any bookshop, any library and you will see dozens of them. They are there because the writers all believe – and usually they are right – that they have something unique to tell us, about their own past lives, a particular remembrance of childhood to express, rare experiences to share.

They are there also because the demand for them is there. Publishers take up such new manuscripts with the eagerness singularly absent from their contemplation of yet another first novel. They mostly differ slightly from one another and yet share a great deal, for the past is to some extent always common ground.

I am talking about those books of reminiscences, the accounts of growing up, most often in the English countryside, certainly before 1939 and sometimes before the 1914–18 War. They have homely titles, and little line drawings to illustrate them, they tell stories which are charming, nostalgic, quaint, and they are often spiced with real sadness and suffering. The message they convey is that things were once like this, and are so no longer, and that that is everyone's loss; they offer a revelation of one corner of Paradise, though they are often down to earth and realistic, too.

If you enjoy them at all, perhaps you do so indiscriminately. I confess that although I like them, the doses have to be small and concentrated. But one or two tower above the rest, to be relished again and again – *Lark Rise to Candleford* is an obvious example, and I have been particularly fond since my own early reading days of Alison Uttley's *The Country Child*.

But it is one other that reigns supreme, for me and for many, a book of the greatest literary merit, a perfect distillation of all its kind, and yet utterly and magnificently itself – Laurie Lee's *Cider with Rosie.* Even the title has a golden halo about it, a short phrase bearing a rich load of meaning and allusion, as a tree bears apples in autumn. Since it was first published over twenty years ago, it has gone through many editions, its fame is worldwide, it has been dramatised, filmed, become a set-textbook for schoolchildren, the subject of research. Yet it survives intact and unspoilt. I find more in it as I grow older; and as the world changes, it has improved with age, acquired deeper subtleties, and some darker overtones, too.

Each time I re-read it, some aspect seems to carry more emphasis, to be charged with a greater meaning, one tiny sentence will spring to my notice and be admired, as when the young Laurie notices the autumnal trees and asks in panic why they are 'falling to bits'.

This time, I cherished best the portrait of Laurie Lee's mother and the passages describing the extremes of summer and winter, for, as he says, 'It becomes increasingly easy in urban life to ignore their extreme humours, but in those days winter and summer dominated our every action, broke into our houses, conscripted our thoughts, ruled our games, and ordered our lives'.

He plunges us into those other-worlds of the respective seasons so that we smell, hear, feel, see, breathe, every detail, in and out of doors.

At the living heart of the book, its lynch-pin and pivot, the focus around which they all live, move and have their being, is Mrs Lee, deserted by her husband but carried forward by eternal hope of his return, mothering in her distracted, abstracted, dedicated way her own sons, and three step-daughters, all crowded in a warm, steamy muddle into the tiny Gloucestershire cottage.

This is a magnificent portrait, loving yet sharp, many-faceted, and it manages to work in three dimensions of time. There is her past, her girlhood and young womanhood, when she was a beauty, in domestic service, enjoying rare moments of personal triumph, driving those around her to affectionate distraction; the 'present', of Laurie's boyhood; and a glimpse, too, of her later years, when she was 'grey . . . and a shade more lightheaded, talking of mansions she would never build', yet not unhappy, not embittered.

There are poignant paragraphs, joyful ones, and hilarious ones, like the account of mother's bicycle riding: 'Happy enough when the thing was in motion, it was stopping and starting that puzzled her. She had to be launched on her way by running parties of villagers and to stop she rode into a hedge'.

It is clear where Laurie got his intelligence, sensitivity, and gifts for seeing, image-making, and responding totally to life. 'Our mother was a buffoon, extravagant and romantic, and was never wholly taken seriously. Yet within her, she nourished a delicacy of taste, a sensibility, a lightness of spirit . . . she loved this world and saw it fresh with hopes that never clouded. She was an artist, a light-giver and an original, and she never for a moment knew it'. And, thanks to her son, she is one of the immortals. We are privileged to know her.

Cider with Rosie is a poet's book *par excellence*, though the language never takes over: Lee does not indulge in lush descriptions for their own sake; the whole has a shape, a backbone, an inner discipline.

It is not a fully documented, chronological autobiography, and that is one of its strengths – too many writers begin at the year 0 and forge relentlessly on to 80. He has selected and crystallised, turned a lantern here and there, not always important or dramatic events and people, except that they seemed so, to a small boy, and remained in his mind and memory.

It is framed by, caught and held between, its opening and closing paragraphs, which are of such simple beauty as takes the breath away. It is a book that, once read, once taken to heart, becomes so much a part of oneself that it is unimaginable that it might never have been written at all, and certainly I cannot conceive of its having been written differently even by so much as the placing of a comma.

(1978)

Under the Greenwood Tree

by Thomas Hardy

In January of this year, the 50th since Thomas Hardy's death, I wrote about *The Return of the Native*, a magnificent but sombre book. Now I come to the year's end and, especially with Christmas almost here, to *Under the Greenwood Tree*, his early novel which is so fitting to the season, partly because its opening pages celebrate the time but mainly because its pure sweetness and light, hope and happiness, humour, merriment and generosity of spirit make it a fine thing to read just now.

Relatively little criticism has been written about it. That is really because there isn't much to say beyond the fact that, in its unique way it is a perfect book. With it, Hardy found his own true voice, as well as the beginnings of fame and success. The novels which follow it provide more food for critics and commentators, because they are denser and far more complex, artistically, intellectually and stylistically, for good or ill.

But here, there is nothing to analyse or unravel, all is as it seems. It has been called Shakespearian, yet every one of Shakespeare's comedies has its dark side, when we are brought up against mortality, human frailty and folly, sadness and loss, if only for a moment. This is not true, just this once, of Hardy. The book follows the fortunes of country characters through the seasons, yet although the aspect of woodland and meadow changes, as it blows bitter cold or dusty hot, rain or fair, the mood does not alter, all is spring and summer at heart.

When critics do turn their attention to *Under the Greenwood Tree* for a short time, even the most rigorous and flinty of them are disarmed. They may begin to glimpse limitations and minor flaws but quickly, and rightly, dismiss them, for they are as nothing in the end, and what has sometimes been seen as a bad break in the book, seems to me a deliberate feature of its construction, and the way form and story reflect one another.

It divides into two halves which make a balanced whole. The first is about the Mellstock Quire, the band of instrumental players and singers who provide the music in the village church. They are richly characterised, full of quirks of personality, behaviour and belief, rooted in the musical, religious and social traditions of their part of England. By the time Hardy was writing, such Quires were extinct; he gives the impression that he speaks of a time which is passing, but in fact it has already passed. The stories, lore and language of these men, who sing 'Remember Adam's Fall' and other obsolete carols, play the brazen serpent and fiddle and despise clarinets, the young Hardy heard from his father and grandfather, both church musicians. He captures convincingly the air of serious purpose with which they go about their Christmas music-making, walking for miles over snow bound fields to sing at every house in the parish, no matter how far-flung. They are proud, dedicated, opinionated, have a strict hierarchy and speak a fruity mixture of Old Testament cadence and Wessex dialect. They are almost, but never quite, caricatures.

And the story is about the end of their world. They are about to be disbanded, by the fresh, young vicar, in favour of an organ played by the new schoolteacher, Miss Fancy Day. It is a potentially poignant event, and later, Hardy would have lent it every tragic under and over-tone; and a shadow would have passed over the earth, leaving us momentarily bleak and cold, if Shakespeare had written it. But here, Hardy deals with the events lightly, deftly, humorously, skating over the thinnest of ice with the fastest blades.

The Mellstock Quire fades out, to make way, in the church and the book, for Fancy Day and her lover, handsome, honest, Dick Dewey. The second part is the story of their romance, whose course runs smoothly, apart from some setbacks barely worth the name. Fancy is a pale, pale sketch for the type of young woman Hardy was to treat in depth and with scorn and severity later. She is a flirt, a tease, rather silly, vain, snobbish and manipulative, leading simple Dick a dance before giving way to his earnest love and good prospects. Poor Dick, we feel, and perhaps we don't care for Fancy and yet, again for the only time in Hardy, there is nothing but joy and married bliss in prospect for the lovers. We don't believe it, not any of it, yet we gladly suspend our own suspicion and cynicism to sour the idyll.

The book is written in the most limpid, graceful and simple prose Hardy probably ever achieved, and it flows out of him like melody. In subsequent novels, he strived so hard to pack in so much, thought deeply and often wanted to impress and sometimes the writing shows the strain. Not here. There is wonderful, spontaneous image-making. 'The limp bacon rasher hung down between the bars of the gridiron like a cat in a child's arms,' and 'a curl of woodsmoke came from the chimney and drooped over the roof like a blue feather in a lady's hat.' His evocation of the great and small beauties of Wessex country, his selective and inventive ear for the rhythms and comedy of rustic speech, his sense of the past, his delight in youthful joy and innocence and old age's ripeness are absolute. Such a world, such unshadowed felicity, may never have existed. No matter. For the time it takes to read *Under the Greenwood Tree*, the vision of Thomas Hardy makes it so.

(1978)

Thomas Hardy

A few years ago, a friend came to ask my advice about her daughter, aged fifteen, who would no longer read anything. She hated books, though she had devoured them voraciously and without much discrimination when younger. Now, her particular aversion was to anything her mother even approved of.

'But she'll listen to you', she said. 'You find the sort of thing she'd like, encourage her. I'm sure you can do something'. I wasn't, but I was flattered and although I disapprove of ramming literature, like food, down unreceptive throats – it usually produces a long-lasting aversion – I thought I might do some successful tempting.

So the girl came to tea a lot and chatted and browsed through my bookshelves, which was the most hopeful sign of all. The genuine, hardened book-hater would never do such a thing. 'Children's books are OK' she said, 'but I'm too old for them now and everything else is so *boring*'.

I worked on that girl hard, I made suggestions, loaned volumes, enlisted aid. No good. All decent literature was 'boring', yet instant paperback pulp was rejected, too. 'Nothing in that. Just silly rubbish'. She wasn't a fool, you see. But after some months, drained of ideas, I gave up in defeat. 'You're just not a reader', I told her. 'You never will be. You'd far better go to the pictures'.

So she did, the following week, to see the film version of *Far from the Madding Crowd*. She came smartly back to my bookshelves.

'That was a fantastic story, I want to read something else by Thomas Hardy.' Her hand hovered over his collected works, stopped at random. 'I'll try this'. It was *The Return of the Native*.

'You won't like . . .'. I bit my tongue. I was supposed to be encouraging her, after all. But I was uneasy. After *Under the Greenwood Tree* this was my own favourite Hardy novel, but I thought of all those aspects of it most likely to frighten away a reluctant reader: the rolling high prose of the opening chapter, full of philosophical and historical diversions, setting the scene on Egdon Heath, obscure biblical and classical allusions, such a barrier, along with their explanatory footnotes, to immediate ease of enjoyment.

It seemed likely that the melodramatic main characters would fail to convince, and sweet Thomasin and faithful Diggory Venn would provoke scorn, while the rustics might be dismissed as Loamshire caricatures. Because I loved the book myself, I felt fiercely protective towards it, yet incapable of putting up a well-argued defence against understandable attack.

I should have foreseen that Hardy's novel and its young reader were well able to take care of themselves. The book was declared the best she'd ever read. It bowled her over and so did the rest of his work, which she went through like an express train. Even the lesser-known and least successful novels like *Two on a Tower*, *The Hand of Ethelberta* and *Laodicean* delighted her. Instinctively, she had approached Hardy the right way – head-on, plunging into the story and simply ignoring surface difficulties.

This year is not only the 150th anniversary of Hardy's death, but the 100th since the publication of *The Return of the Native* and, remembering how it had marked such a turning-point in the intellectual life of one young woman (who, at twenty-five, is still reading Hardy and much else), I returned to it myself, after an absence of some years, and fell under its powerful sway once again.

Above all, though, I now understand completely why the girl was won over by it. It is one of the two great English novels most likely to succeed with adolescents because it treats of emotions, moods and behaviour which they are in the middle of experiencing themselves, and because those are so dramatically emphasised. The other book is *Wuthering Heights*, to which I was passionately addicted at the age of fifteen, and with which I am now quite out of patience, for although both writers appeal to adolescents, Hardy was altogether a mature adult, whose qualities impress one with increasing force over the years, whereas the Emily Brontë of *Wuthering Heights* was an adolescent herself in temperament, in love with her own hero, and the bleak moorlands.

Hardy maintains an intelligent detachment, although, in describing Egdon Heath, he was writing about the place he knew and cared for best, for he grew up in its shadow, his earliest memories were of its sights and seasons. Yet he allows his characters to feel violently towards it, either in love or hatred.

If you respond to landscape at all when young, it is likely to be in some bleak, forbidding, uncompromising place like the Wessex Heathland, just as you identify with, while despising Eustacia Vye's personality, her self-conscious solitariness, restless dissatisfaction and morbidity, her night-walks and broodings.

Eustacia believes in Love, and wills herself into it, and if young women can love Heathcliff, how much more does Thomas Hardy offer them – a trio of fatally attractive heroes: Damon Wildeve, gambler and flirt, the attractive rotter; Clym Yeobright who, apart from his irresistible moral loftiness, goes blind – something guaranteed to draw women towards him in devoted pity; and homely, trusty Diggory Venn, so devoted in love that he selflessly furthers a rival claim because it also furthers his love's joy.

Tragedy and melodrama, so beloved of adolescents, link hands when Eustacia and Wildeve plunge to their deaths in the foaming weir after a night of Lear-like tempest on the heath, and, because Hardy had to satisfy contemporary serial-story readers against his own better judgment, he also satisfies youthful desires for calm after the storm, when Justice dances together with Happiness, as Diggory at last wins his reward for faithfulness, in married love.

I do not wish to trivialise Hardy by high-lighting certain limited facets of his appeal. But the point is that he is both a mighty novelist and a genuinely popular one, read with devotion by many to whom the word 'classic' is anathema. I was surprised only last week by the enthusiasm of an unbookish nineteen-year-old girl for *Jude the Obscure*, a novel I have never cared for.

Hardy was the last of the Victorians and the first of the moderns, bestriding both centuries and embracing a greater variety of readers than perhaps any other English writer.

(1978)

The Pilgrim's Progress

by John Bunyan

I can remember most vividly that it was a warm Sunday evening in early June and that I was sitting beside an open window smelling wallflowers and new-mown grass and hearing a swing creak, when I opened a small book bound in olive green and read, 'As I walked through the wilderness of this world, I lighted on a certain place, where was a den; and I laid me down in that place to sleep, and as I slept I dreamed a dream'.

My book was *The Pilgrim's Progress*, I was nine years old, and I had never been so utterly possessed by the other worlds of a man's imagination. I saw, heard, smelled everything in the places described there, I felt overcome by dread and horror, shame and determination, hope and joy. Yet I do not think my experience was at all an unusual one.

It is 500 years since John Bunyan first published his story of Christian's journey, after he fled his home in the City of Destruction, and went through the wicket gate and on towards Mount Sion. Since then, tens of thousands of men, women and children of all creeds and classes and educational levels have been held in thrall by it, its inspiration has been second only to that of the Bible; the extreme beauty of the prose has burned itself upon their memories, and the saltiness of the characterisation, the pithiness of much of the dialogue, struck familiar chords in their own experience, however limited.

It was not particularly written for children, and nowadays, like so much literature of its kind, it is scarcely read at all by them, but those who have always thought of it as a children's classic are not quite wrong, nor was I very precocious. It is a book which works on many levels, and grows up with one.

Its prime appeal is as a story, an ongoing adventure; what happens next is all important, and those happenings are exciting and dramatic, and contrast strongly with one another. And however easy any child may find it to concentrate, he needs diversity, movement, and progress in his reading matter.

Bunyan is never boring, because his digressions are either short and entertaining in themselves, or else they are self-contained – recapitulations, or conversations about one aspect of religion or morality – and may easily be skipped without detriment to the narrative. But above all, he had the gift that is worth everything – the ability to conjure up those other worlds, in which we too may live. The atmosphere of the Valley of the Shadow of Death or the dungeons of Doubting Castle cling about one like a fog, that of the Delectable Mountains is sweet, and there is a shock that strikes cold to the heart when, after the cackle and dazzle of the city called Vanity Fair, Faithful is tried and summarily put to death. These are scenes which, once read, become part of those underground caverns of the imagination forever.

The same is true of the prose, which has its roots in the Authorised Version that Bunyan knew so well, and rings with its cadences, and yet which is also full of plain 17th-century English as it must have been spoken, sprinkled with country similes and homely aphorisms.

The saying that 'the devil has all the best tunes' applies scarcely at all to *The Pilgrim's Progress*. The giants, hypocrites and fools are brilliantly characterised and immensely diverting, but the hero, Christian, is no vapid, symbolic figure. He makes mistakes, looks silly, feels chastened; his wife, whose pilgrimage takes up Part II, has all the familiar characteristics of wives, mothers, neighbours. Perhaps I was a little disappointed in Bunyan's Heaven when young, not understanding how he, like every other writer of his time, was forced to fall back upon stock Biblical metaphor to describe the indescribable – on golden crowns and pavements, harps and white raiments. Yet how gloriously his prose rises, as he fills it with the music of the Heavenly city, the bells and trumpets and songs.

When I first read the story I committed whole sections to memory without realising that I was doing so, so that the book has influenced and pervaded and enriched me ever since.

It is adults who appreciate the human and social subtleties of Bunyan, a shrewd commentator who reveals, in character sketches, dialogue and brilliant name-calling, a clear-eyed knowledge of men, their minds and manners. But adults have to 'become as little children' in order to reach the heart of the book, for it is children who understand Bunyan's straightforwardness and simple moral purpose. *The Pilgrim's Progress* is not a novel, nor was it meant primarily as any work of art, whether fable, romance or allegory. It was written by a teacher and preacher, committed to what he believed was the truth and imprisoned for his public witness to it.

But, paradoxically, it is not a sermon, and would never have enjoyed popularity and influence as such. It succeeds, like all parables, by the very fact of it being a fiction.

(1978)

Beatrix Potter

Even if my daughter Jessica, aged ten months, eventually reacts against a literary household, at the moment she loves books; she gets excited when she sees them, sits patiently trying to turn only one page at a time, so anxious to decipher both pictures and print. In the light of this, we are building up a library for her, and so I have been much occupied lately with the perusal of children's literature.

Occasionally, I look well ahead, to the time when she can read herself. But for the next few years, she will be looking and listening; this is the age of pictures and rhymes, of alphabets and repetition, merging into the first enjoyment of complete stories. All of it depends on parental participation, and although I can get pleasure from the bold, bright illustrations of Dick Bruna or Richard Scarry, and don't at all mind reading board books called *Animal Friends* or *Happy Days*, their appeal is limited. Which is partly why, last week, I re-read all the works of Beatrix Potter, wondering how early they can be introduced. For they were my own first 'proper' books, and now I see that they are both old-fashioned, of their own time, and timeless, like all great works of art.

Miss Potter herself would have been as scathing of attempts to rate her books among the classics as she was to anyone who compared her watercolours to the work of the major English landscape painters. She thought she knew her own limitations and so, in a way, she did.

Her world was as small and confined as that of a miniaturist, bounded by here a hedge, there a gate or a garden path, and she never attempted to stride out beyond it. But her world is a microcosm, and what she did, she did perfectly.

I have gone through these tales of rabbits and mice, squirrels, hedgehogs, foxes and badgers, and been both enchanted all over again by the familiar scenes, and newly appreciative of the richness of invention and language, the details and the humour. Here is everything a child could want and more, at the beginning of a lifetime of reading.

As much as anything, it is a question of the author's attitude and its accompanying tone. Mainly, it is clear and direct, but it also contains some uncompromising words or phrases which prove unfamiliar and difficult to a child. 'Nutkin was excessively impertinent in his manners', and 'Hunca Munca had a frugal mind'. 'Tom Kitten was affronted'. Children will usually ask the meanings of such words, but sometimes they deliberately do not, preferring either to guess – which is excellent, like stretching up to something just out of reach, or else to leave the long words untranslated and retaining their mysterious, incantatory properties.

Otherwise, these are plain tales, both adventurous and soothingly domestic and full of those precise details which the young require to know. A packet of tea, a pound of lump sugar and a pot of marmalade. There are one or two chilling touches of the macabre – the descriptions of Mr Tod's kitchen at dusk, or the chimney and attic hideouts of *Samuel Whiskers*, in both of which preparations are being made to kill, cook, and eat young animals. But for the most part, things are as sunny as a spring morning.

Like many of the best children's books, the tales are anthropomorphic; we learn an awful lot about the quirks and charms of human personality and behaviour from these four-legged creatures in blue jackets, starched white aprons or galoshes. Beatrix Potter observed animals closely and lovingly and she got their characters exactly right.

The best way to acquire an ear, and so a love for English prose, is to absorb its rhythms unconsciously at an early age, and especially through these stories, so gracefully are they written, with such economy and ease, the lines pointed up with wit and admonition and perfect adjectives. As they become familiar, over many readings, they are committed to heart and memory. I shall be able to recite Peter Rabbit to my daughter, it is as though I was born knowing it.

Occasionally when the author intrudes into the narrative, the tone becomes arch, but never once sentimental – all the truths about wildlife are here, the terrors, fights and killings. Beatrix Potter was a realist, as she was also a moralist. Naughtiness may be understood. It is never condoned. Flopsy, Mopsy and Cotton Tail, who were good little rabbits, ate bread and milk, and blackberries for supper, but Peter was dosed with camomile tea. This is the world of the Victorian nursery.

It is also Victorian rural England, which has vanished. Of course there are still moors and fells, kitchen gardens, woods and ponds, but they are fewer, and life in them is faster and noisier, the details of domesticity have changed – no creaking carts, cool dairies and goffering irons.

Within these pages, Jessica will be able to breathe the air of the country as it was in her own grandmother's childhood, and understand how times were then, for as these small, fictional animals lived, so did the people.

'The countryside?' Miss Potter herself wrote, 'that pleasant, unchanging world of realism and romance which in our northern clime is stiffened by hard weather, a tough ancestry and the strength that comes from the hills'.

If that is the foundation of my daughter's literary inheritance, what could be better?

(1978)

The Far Cry

by Emma Smith

I do not linger over secondhand bookstalls as I used to; some other business always presses and our shelves already overflow. But I usually dive in for five minutes and, once in a while, pull out a plum, something out of print and long sought after, never worth much money but valuable to me.

Twenty years ago, when I was about to publish my own first novel, at a tender age, I was told of a similar young woman who had written one which had been widely and loudly acclaimed and sold well. But she had produced nothing else and the book had dropped out of sight. Last month I finally tracked it down. I gave ten pence to the funds of a school in Woodstock for a good, clean copy of *The Far Cry* by Emma Smith (Macgibbon & Kee, 1949). I had no idea what it was about or would be like but I have a certain missionary zeal for resurrecting novels which deserve a new readership and even, with luck, a new edition. So many appear and disappear like shooting stars and most deserve oblivion, but a few are worthy of a permanent place in print. What, I wondered, of Emma Smith? I expected to find a work of promise which might betray its author's youthfulness, and seem dated. I did not expect to discover a small masterpiece. I began it with interest, and read on with growing amazement, deepening admiration. There is nothing 'promising' about it, it is a completely formed, satisfying work of art, rich in human understanding and all manner of subtleties, beautifully shaped, evocative, moving and mature.

It seems to have been written out of a long lifetime of quiet, penetrating observation and experience of a wide variety of human beings, their personalities, emotions and behaviour.

Teresa Digby is her father's second child, by his second disastrous marriage, and is living with a well-meaning but narrow aunt when her mother threatens to reappear and lay claim to her. To her surprise – for she has never been close to him – Randall Digby carries her off in panic to India and his elder daughter, Ruth, married to a tea-planter. In her presence, he is sure, all will come right, for Ruth is good, true and wise beyond description, the shining light at the end of her father's tormented journey with this awkward younger child he neither knows nor likes. Teresa is not pretty, not graceful, not sensible, she 'sticks out like pins at every angle', and throughout their passage to India by boat and hot, slow train, her presence is an irritant and an embarrassment both to her father and to her own self.

This is a most telling portrait of an intelligent, sensitive girl growing up, reminiscent of the young Portia in Elizabeth Bowen's *The Death of the Heart.* Emma Smith's novel echoes those of several other writers, without being, in any sense, derivative. She writes of English people journeying to India, and its impact upon them, so vividly that not just sights, but sounds, smells, whole atmospheres, rise off the page, and it is not merely that her subject-matter and setting are rather Forsterian; she uses simile and symbol in her way, investing certain places and incidents with far more than their immediate and obvious significance.

Yet, just like E. M. Forster, she never spells her meanings out, is never pedestrian, only, with the instinct of a novelist born, lets them stand by themselves, to be given weight, and interpreted, by the reader. There are some magnificent set-pieces of description – a Hindu Festival of Light, a river picnic, Teresa's night encounter with a tiger. Above all, though, this is an intricate study of human nature. It is about growing up, and disillusionment, pride, pretence and vanity, and the suffering they cause; for Ruth turns out to be only a poor sham of an angel. It is about simple, clear-eyed love – that of Ruth's husband, a good man.

A great deal happens to the protagonists, which advances them along the road of self-knowledge and self-acceptance, and so, in turn, understanding of others. Teresa suffers shock after shock and emerges bruised, yet stronger and wiser. Her father dies, her sister dies, the one still in ignorance of most of the truth about himself, about his daughters and life in general. But Ruth has just begun to learn, and to repent. Their deaths mean freedom for Teresa and Edwin, though they barely recognise the fact. Yet it is a hopeful novel, positive and liberating, on the side of life and goodness, permeated with all the humane values.

The prose is a joy to read, accomplished and graceful, the confident writing of a natural stylist, and there are some passages of great beauty.

I was bemused by the novel whilst reading it and it has occupied my thoughts considerably since. From it, I have learned a good many things about the art of fiction. Yet I am taken aback by the sheer accident of my finding it at all. How many people ought to be reading it too; how few can do so.

But there is something in the air. I now discover that, after thirty years, Emma Smith will publish a new novel this autumn. Perhaps the event will encourage someone to re-issue her first. Its rescue from the relative oblivion of secondhand stalls is long overdue.

(1978)

Toad of Toad Hall

by A. A. Milne

On the Saturday after Christmas we went to the theatre. It was my annual treat – or rather, as my husband qualifies, my annual pilgrimage. Now, I am not very good at the theatre. I grow bored and restless. I do not care for histrionics or to be harrowed, harangued or embarrassed in public. I prefer to stay at home with a book or, if I am in the mood for drama, with the script of a television or radio play.

In his impoverished student days, my husband spent his pittance on theatre tickets rather than food, and he is the man who has not missed a single Shakespeare production at Stratford in twenty years, so it is fortunate that our marriage rests on a surer foundation than a mutual taste for play-going. Yet at this season, he cheerfully pays for the best stalls seats, not to mention chocolates, ices and souvenir programmes, knowing that he can relax in the certain knowledge that this is one occasion when I shall not leave the performance at the first interval, but remain by his side to cry 'Encore' at the bitter end.

The play? Why, what else but that most magical of all adaptations from a classic book, A. A. Milne's *Toad of Toad Hall*. The moment I think of it, I begin to wax lyrical, for I was raised on it, the play and its original, Kenneth Grahame's *The Wind in the Willows* went hand in hand with me through my early childhood, and each has enhanced and enriched the other over the years. I cannot remember which came first for me, and certainly cannot say which I love best – nor does it matter one jot.

Clearly, though, a gentleman sitting near to us in The Old

Vic last week felt otherwise, for he lectured his companions loudly and vigorously on the subject. 'Not a patch on the book', he said, 'Now if you read that, you will find that X and Y happen, and there is a character X . . . The play is shorter, and altogether more simplistic . . . it is bolder and cruder in its characterisation, there isn't the verbal subtlety at all . . . and such and such a scene isn't even in the book . . . and what happened to that long, lyrical interlude when . . . this is a *sketch* of the book'.

Quite, I almost said over his shoulder, exactly so, you have got the whole point. The adaptation is *not* the book, does not pretend to be the book, it is in a different medium, written for different circumstances. Of course there are never so many verbal felicities, stylistic intricacies, slow, detailed descriptions and repetitions in a play, of course the outline is simpler, there is more emphasis on plot and pace and a few, dominant character traits.

I have a treasured first edition of *Toad of Toad Hall*, published exactly fifty years ago, in which A. A. Milne sets out the aims and problems of the adapter with clarity and sensitivity. His devoted admiration for the original text is explicit, his awareness of the demands of the playhouse acute, and after stating some of the difficulties that faced him, he writes modestly, 'I have, I hope, made some sort of entertainment, with enough of Kenneth Grahame in it to appease his many admirers and enough of me in it to justify my name upon the title page'.

Yes. For every true adaptation is also a new creation, at least in part; this is an art, not merely copying or transferring and the imprint of the adapter's creative imagination should be clearly recognisable.

What is it, then, about Toad? Why do I see some production of it every year without fail? Why does it still enchant, excite, interest, intrigue and satisfy me? Nostalgia? Oh, no, much more.

I can make out a good case for its being the archetypal drama. It contains elements of everything one requires from a play, or a dramatic entertainment, call it what you will.

The appeal of it is that of all such anthropomorphic stories written since time began; it mirrors another, smaller, animal world, which fascinates us – though why we should want to see rats, badgers, toads and moles behaving utterly like themselves and also like human characters, I do not know. We just do.

It is perfect English pastoral. The river bank is a paradise into which we can enter, for a time, through the illusion of the play; when the gauze curtain shifts, so that Marigold's fantasy comes true, then all our childhood dreams and inventions and wishes appear before us, true for that time, also. Then, it fades, reality takes us over once more and the resulting melancholy is poignant. Yet one would have it no other way. The dream must fade and we must wake, the gauze curtain drops down.

There is every kind of humour, slapstick, verbal, practical-jokey, situation-comical. There are all the elements of pantomime . . . a talking horse, transfiguration scenes, funny disguises. There is romping, fighting, singing and dancing – for the H. Fraser Simpson music is an indispensable part of the play. There is also some real terror; the stoats and weasels, haunting Toad and poor, confused Mole, lost in the Wild Wood, can be very frightening indeed. These are the villains, who get their come uppance, defeated by our Heroes. And the Hero Himself (for Toad is, of course, just that) has to learn some salutary lessons, before triumphing once more – this, like all good plays, has a moral.

For adult sophisticates there are various literary and dramatic parallels, strong echoes of Shakespearian scenes and of Gilbertian parody.

There are quiet moments when you can hear a pin drop in the theatre, and others when you can't hear yourself think; there are plenty of occasions for audience participation of the right kind ('Look out, he's behind you!') and even a little love interest; pompous authority is made to look foolish, yet right and order prevail. The ending is happy, yet curiously sad. And there are enough character-types for us to find our identification.

I come out of Toad every year, feeling content and that the world is an altogether better place for its existence. I am a better and happier person for having seen it again. I also come out and return to Kenneth Grahame's book, with renewed delight, which is exactly what Milne would have wanted.

Above all, I am overjoyed that each new generation of children take the book and the play to their hearts. Even my daughter, Jessica, who, at two-and-a-half, cannot understand the narrative or yet go to the play, knows the story through E. H. Shepard's lovely illustrations – she, too, is already in thrall to my most precious Otherworld.

(1978)

Charles Dickens

If, as I firmly believe, the most valuable and meaningful, and most welcome praise and appreciation a writer can receive is that of his fellow artists, whether contemporaries or successors, then Charles Dickens stands crowned above all English novelists and for all time.

Every writer I know refers to him with the deepest respect and singles him out, more often than any other, for admiration. Most will gladly acknowledge a debt to him, too, though it may be only a general one, for if you know and love Dickens and you are a novelist yourself, you cannot help but learn from him about more aspects of the art than will ever be superficially apparent. He has such a powerful spirit and it is all-pervading; his influence is the best kind, because it goes deep. In his own day, he may well have been widely limited in matters of style and construction and choice of subject matter, but that is no longer true. Now, we can only gasp at his genius and despair of there ever again being a novelist to come within a hundred miles of his greatness, while at the same time acknowledging him as a source.

Dickens is taken seriously, keenly valued and minutely studied. He is also, thank heavens, still hugely enjoyed; did ever a novelist give such pure delight, pleasure, entertainment – call it what you will? The more I come to understand just how mighty his talent was, the greater significance his work has for me, the more I also revel in him as I dive deep down into the books again and again.

I have done so since I was nine years old, when I inherited from my great-uncle the Complete Works, bound in brown leatherette and smelling of must, the pages tallow, with rust-spotted margins. It is a poor, cheap edition, the print smudged and the Phiz illustrations dark because of over-used plates, the text is hopelessly unscholarly, yet I love it. It is the edition I always read from, though I may refer to others.

It seems that an early and delighted absorption in his novels, consolidated in later life by that closer study of them which is guided and illuminated by good teachers and critics, is what most commonly makes 'a Dickensian'. Yet, it is never too late, and I am a passionate advocate of the second try most particularly where Dickens is concerned, for too many have been put off by the wrong book at the wrong age.

And it still happens. I know young people, readers all of them, lovers of Thomas Hardy and the Brontës, as well as more contemporary literature, who jeer and sneer at Dickens and are amazed at one's love and high estimation of his work. It saddens rather than angers me, though I am prepared to justify my admiration and defend the novels, on any critical front, against all comers. But most people have simply missed the point because they are unacquainted with the best.

They were usually dragged by the nose unwillingly through *A Tale of Two Cities*, that totally uncharacteristic, artificial piece, or *David Copperfield*, which I truly believe you cannot understand when very young, even though it is *about* the very young. Yet it is still taught in schools, often in dreadful, bowdlerised versions.

Nor does *The Pickwick Papers*, that unsophisticated picaresque, seem funny to most who read it early, but tediously quaint, dated and irrelevant, all jolly fat Christmas-card men in gaiters, on coaches. Young readers want to commit themselves, their imaginations and emotions, hearts and consciences, to a novel. They respond to Dickens's passionate defence of suffering individuals, his virulent hatred of injustice and snobbery, cant and hypocrisy, of 'the insolence of office and the law's delay', his satiric attacks on hidebound, monolithic institutions and cold-hearted men.

Deep love and friendship, fear and violence, a strong, vividly evoked atmosphere, a dramatic and eventful plot, grotesque humour and macabre characters and happenings – all these things are what Dickens is about, as he is also about morality and politics; he is a poet, and a stylist who carries you along on the deep-sea rhythms of his prose, a writer who experimented with and stretched the language to its boundaries, mined all its richness and complexity and harnessed it to work for him. His imagination burns and blazes, the power of his vision seizes and invades you, his endless inventiveness is dazzling.

First-time readers, and those who once made an unfortunate false start with Dickens, cannot fail to respond to some or all of these aspects of his books, if only they open themselves up to them, and if only they read the best novels. Once you have been won over by these, by *Bleak House* and *Little Dorrit*, *Dombey and Son* and *Hard Times* and, greatest of all, *Our Mutual Friend*, the time has come to go back to the early work. For I am beginning to believe that it takes the maturest and most experienced taste to appreciate Dickens's first novels.

I cannot separate myself into reader and writer; what Dickens does for the one is what influences the other. It is from this way of looking at and then re-creating the world, in his own idiosyncratic pattern and design, that one learns so much; there is an artistic and a human purpose in it and the two are interdependent.

He bores to the heart of things, enlarges, illumines, reveals, makes utterly clear and freshly comprehensible. But above all what affects one so is the intense excitement he generates in putting his imaginative vision on to the page, so that it throws off sparks which somehow catch light within oneself. What he does, I want to do, infected by his passion and intensity, though in my own way, not in his. That is the real inspiration one artist can be to another.

(1979)

My Family and Other Animals

by Gerald Durrell

I sometimes need a book to fit a particular situation. So, before we embarked recently on the traumatic and protracted business of house-moving, I searched along the fast-emptying shelves for exactly the right one to see me through. I wanted a book that was light of heart, full of gentle, warm humour, but not *just* a funny book; one with a wide variety of characters, which would interest and inform me, and transplant me, too, away from tea-chests and curtainless windows.

Above all, it must be familiar and arranged so that I could extract fairly self-contained episodes, to finish at a sitting.

It took scarcely any time for the perfect answer to present itself, and I secured Gerald Durrell's *My Family and Other Animals* to my person, against the upheaval ahead.

I'm sure you can imagine what a boon it proved; how I wrapped kitchen-ware with one hand while rocking with new delight over the scene with the escaping scorpions, sat on floorboards in rooms empty of furniture yet filled with the personalities of Spiro and Theo and Yani, the cackle of Alecko and the Magenpies echoing down the stairs; how, very late one night I came with a glad cry to the chapter in which the glow-worms and the phosphorescent porpoises are so evocatively described . . . And do you recall how Mother and Margo . . .

There I go, running on ahead and falling into the trap. For I have so often been infuriated by those people who talk in a kind of short-hand about books they know well, sharing episodes, leaving sentences half-finished because a reference is at once picked up by a fellow devotee, who tosses back a quotation in response. And I have been guilty of it myself, talking about the Jeeves books of P. G. Wodehouse with a friend, in an elliptical manner, punctuated by fits of giggles, which is quite incomprehensible to outsiders.

In fact, what I most want to do with the books, like Durrell's, which I know and love, is to introduce them to the whole world, so that everyone can be an insider. Sadly, one's enthusiasm is not always infectious, and others remain stubbornly unconvinced. It is hardest of all with humour. I have often failed with Wodehouse and E. F. Benson, just as Firbank fans fail with me.

But Durrell never fails, for the charm of *My Family and Other Animals* lies in far more than its humour, which pulses through the body of the book, but is never obtrusive – joke for joke's sake.

It is a glorious story, and a true one, about the springtime of Gerald's life, when he and his family 'fled from the gloom of the English summer like a flock of migrating swallows' to the magical island of Corfu. 'The family' are the heart and core of the book. Into their dotty, squabbling, variegated net are drawn, for life or fleetingly, other characters, mainly Corfiotes, and a menagerie, acquired all by Gerry, odd creatures from odd sources – a vicious, black-backed gull given to him by a convict on parole, a young Scops owl, rescued from an olive-tree hole, stray dogs called Widdle and Puke, two magpies, a giant tortoise.

With all of them, as with Mother and Margo, Larry (Lawrence) and Leslie, we become intimate. Mother is the linch-pin of family and story, a gifted cook and gardener, tolerant and vague, forever deciding where she wants to be buried, forever teetering on the verge of insolvency. Leslie hunts animals. Larry writes, of course, and has sophisticated friends.

His luggage consists of crates of books, a typewriter and a briefcase of clothes. Margo's 'contained a multitude of diaphanous garments, three books on slimming, and a regiment of small bottles each containing some elixir guaranteed to cure acne'. The relationship between them and Gerry, the narrator, is a mixture of fondness, fury and bewilderment. He is a born naturalist, viewing with incomprehension those who do not share his passion for all creatures great and small. He has the dedicated patience and inquisitiveness of the professional and a disarming lack of concern for others' phobias. He puts scorpions into match-boxes and water-snakes into the bath. Larry regards him rather as Robert Brown regarded his brother, William.

The narrative simply follows the fortunes of the family, as they move, for rather arbitrary reasons, around the island from the strawberry-pink, to daffodil-yellow, to snow-white villa, having crises and parties, making friends, friends, friends; Spiro, the taxi-driver, and Mr Fix-it who talks wonderful Greek-American, Theodore, Gerry's teacher-naturalist, stammering with shyness and excitement about the world about him, the Rose-beetle man, a travelling Papageno of the mountain roads.

Durrell writes quite beautifully, especially of summer nights, drenched in scents, moonlight, wine, cicadas. The atmosphere of Corfu washes over and envelops you, and though I am sure it is all changed, all lost, no matter. It is still a paradise, pinned down forever between the covers of Durrell's glorious book, like one of the butterflies he found and caught there.

(1979)

Wide Sargasso Sea

by Jean Rhys

I embarked upon my re-reading of the Brontës, with *Jane Eyre*, but then, instead of stepping forwards, to *Shirley* and *Villette*, or even sideways to the novels of Emily and Ann, I took a line which runs up to and away from *Jane Eyre*, parallel with it, and in and out of it – I returned to that landmark of post-war fiction, *Wide Sargasso Sea*, by Jean Rhys, who died earlier this year. Her extraordinary novel, about Mr Rochester's mad wife, is not the only book I can think of which springs directly out of another, but it is certainly most rare in that it both stands in its own right, as a great work of the literary imagination, *and* adds a new dimension to the book which inspired it.

It is not merely a gloss on *Jane Eyre*, it enhances, echoes and illuminates it, explains, qualifies and even changes it – or rather, changes our attitude to its characters and their story. You can perfectly well read each book independently, yet a reading of both together is an infinitely more rewarding and subtle experience.

I found myself thinking of *Jane Eyre* less in terms of its author than of the Victorian novel and the social and intellectual climate in which it was written, the family circumstances out of which all the Brontë genius sprang, and more and more in relation to Jean Rhys and her particular talent, background and literary personality. To do this to *Jane Eyre* is perhaps to uproot it from its native soil and culture, but that, temporarily, is an excellent thing, not only because, as a result, it shines quite differently, like a jewel in a new setting, but also because a view of literature and art which is always tied to one country, one tradition, has a most restricting, claustrophobic effect upon the reader.

I have known purists, Brontë devotees, who overcame an initial resistance to the very idea of *Wide Sargasso Sea*, and were both totally converted to it, as a fine novel, and acknowledged its enrichment of their understanding and love of its original. I have also, incidentally, known those whose sympathies and tastes were most decidedly biased in favour of contemporary writers, and who had perhaps been put off *Jane Eyre* – and many another 19th-century novel – in their youth, won over and stimulated by Jean Rhys to a re-reading and re-assessment of it. To their surprise, they found Charlotte Brontë's classic story a quite different book from the one they half-remembered, more exciting, challenging, adult and, most remarkable of all, more 'modern'.

I have to confess my own lack of sympathy with the rest of Jean Rhys's work. I can admire the early novels detachedly, see that they are superior to much modern fiction written by and about women, and that they are remarkably ahead of their time – the 1920s and '30s – in technical assurance, confidence and control. Yet I do not care for those taut, neurotic, ultimately self-pitying tales of depressed heroines suffering, starving, in bars, cafés and sleazy lodging-houses in Paris and London, oppressed by, yet parasites upon, men. Moreover, they lack the vital spark of imaginative genius, they are still tied to earth and autobiography, to real experience described economically and vividly, but not transformed and transmuted by the creative genius. It took *Jane Eyre*, with which Jean Rhys had been obsessed all her life, to free her, so that the kite of her imagination soared. Also she went back, not into her immediate past, but to her childhood, shaping-place and treasure-house of all art.

Mr Rochester's mad wife, locked in the attic at Thornfield Hall, was born in the Caribbean. So was Jean Rhys. She spent her first sixteen years in Dominica, then left it forever, and it haunted her, and also remained intact within her, sealed off like a capsule. By the time she came to write about it, and to tell how Rochester married his poor, mad girl, to give us her story, her memories of that place had been changed, worked upon, lent symbolic significance, by time, and her own later experience. She identified with Mrs Rochester, the capsule broken open, reality became art, memory was changed into imaginative truth.

Wide Sargasso Sea is an unforgettable novel. It is full of the sinister beauty and dramatic impact of the Caribbean Island, colours, scents, sounds, weather, and, above all, people. Its place may be, at least until the very end of the book, quite different from the England of *Jane Eyre*, but the novelist's *sense* of that place is equally strong and vividly conveyed. Like *Jane Eyre*, it is a passionate novel, full of wild emotion, just held in check by the artist's controlling hand; here are the extremes of sexuality, insanity, terror, hatred, the domination of one personality by another, pulling below the book's surface like currents, erupting into dramatic, even melodramatic action – yet within the context of these characters and their circumstances, it is always entirely credible and convincing.

On the surface perhaps, and at a first reading, it might not seem to have so very much in common with *Jane Eyre* as we gradually realise is the case – for what completely different women these writers were, how totally disparate their lives and times. Yet were they? There is a powerful common artistic identity between them, which a study of both their novels and their lives, makes plain.

I have been taken to task recently, for appearing to question the value of the study of artists' lives, but I was, of course, condemning cults of personality which exclude the works, and the sensationalising of intimate details. Serious biographies of writers are important, as revelations of unique human beings, and for the illumination they throw on their books, and the production of them. Knowing somehing about Jean Rhys and Charlotte Brontë enriches our understanding of their novels, just as those novels in their turn complement and cross-fertilise one another, until the stature of both is greatly raised.

(1979)

Our Mutual Friend

by Charles Dickens

To return to Dickens and to that finest novel of them all, *Our Mutual Friend* . . . To some extent, no matter how rigorous one's training in critical impartiality, one still bases value judgments upon personal taste. So, I enjoy this book, its imagery and characters, atmosphere, tone and narrative style, its flavour, all speak most deeply to me and find echoes in my own imagination.

But I do also believe it to be his greatest book, and I am by no means alone, although it was much misunderstood in Dickens's own day, and is still less popular and familiar among general readers than, say, *Great Expectations* or *David Copperfield*. But those who love it, love it well indeed, and although it is not exactly typical Dickens, I would always recommend it to a beginner, because it is so haunting and powerful and unusual, and also because it is least flawed by sentimentality or patches of sagging invention.

Our Mutual Friend is a dark book, its images are sinister and sombre. At the heart of it, and in and out of all its veins and arteries runs the river, the muddy, seeping, sweeping, swirling Thames and its tributaries. Many of its characters' lives revolve about its wharves, under its bridges, among rotting wet wood and rope and all the detritus of the tides. It opens with a corpse being dragged from the water, other men are drowned before the end; and the corpse floats us straight to the core of the mystery and puzzle, one of double-identity, disappearance, masquerade and confusion, around which the complex, multi-stranded plot ravels and unravels.

It certainly defies synopsis, and if I cannot give a brief

resumé of what happens, nor can I briefly say what the novel is *about*, because, like all Dickens's books, it is about almost everything in the world, every aspect of human affairs, both individual and social. I can only pick out a few ingredients with which to arouse the interest and excitement of new readers and stir the memories of old. And it *is* an exciting book, I recall that, just glancing through the names . . . Rogue Riderhood, Mortimer Lightwood, Bradley Headstone, Mr Twemlow, Fascination Fledgby, the Podsnaps, the Veneerings.

Principally, the book is about money and its effect on those who covet, get, hoard or squander it, distort its importance, and the appalling consequences of its misuse and, worse, its complete absence. Money is snobbery and show, power and temptation, it changes men into monsters and slaves, it is dust – but it is also a transforming agent – dust turns to gold, want to plenty, it may be, in the right hands, an instrument of happiness and delight. Dickens is making a careful distinction. He was a realist and he did not despise material comforts.

Scene after scene make a lasting impact, but the characters are even more impressive, because they go so deep, they are psychologically intricate and convincing, though there are the familiar comics and grotesques, too – sharp-tongued, crippled Jenny Wren, the doll's dressmaker, and Mr Venus, who deals in human bones and skulls and jars of pickled foetuses.

But little is superficial. Bradley Headstone, the proud school-master, is a terrifying study of a man consumed and driven to madness, violence and self-destruction by that obsessive, passionate love which is akin to hate, and there are numerous subtle portraits of deceit, of self and others, and duplicity, for this is a book full of masks and faces, seeming and being. The simple direct characters are few, the good characters believable; Lizzie Hexam is a rare, successful example of the good, faithful, loving, beautiful young woman.

Dickens worms his way under the skin of those who would keep their motives and doings most to themselves, whose lives are taken up with concealment and evasion, and exposes them. We see them as they are at the glittering dinner party, and in the hostile privacy of the marital chamber. He is more coldly ruthless with them, and more cunning in his own plottings and manipulation, more virulent in his championing of those he holds up as an example to us, than anywhere else in his work, and his touch is entirely assured.

I do not want to imply that all is bleakness and bitterness. There is love, between father and child, brother and sister, friends, as well as between men and women as sexual creatures, and there is comedy, too, but, like that of Shakespeare's late plays, it is muted, and there is an edge to it. We can laugh at the pretentious antics and airs of Mrs Wilfer, but cannot forget that she is both fool and tyrant, who has made the life of her gentle husband a misery and turned one, and nearly two, daughters into wayward, self-absorbed images of herself.

Our Mutual Friend is all of a piece, caught up and bound together in a unity of vision; every scene and character, every ramification of the plot, every minute detail, partakes of and contributes to the whole, nothing is incongruous, there is no imbalance and we are not let down at any point. The only other novel in which the vision is so sustained, the metaphor so complete, is *Little Dorrit*. But in the end, I do not find that book so powerful, so gripping and affecting, terrifying and fascinating as *Our Mutual Friend*.

(1979)

The Smaller Sky

by John Wain

In the world of the weekly book review pages, novels are treated, at least by implication, as news, and one of the more regrettable results of this is that the same thing happens to many of them as happens to the actual news items . . . they pass quickly out of notice and are forgotten, overtaken by the ever encroaching tide of the next batch, and the next . . .

Of course some survive for rather longer in the public attention, either because they (or, more likely, their authors) attract a lot of publicity of one kind or another, because they reach the best seller lists or, rarely, because they are novels of importance and worth, destined to take their place in the history of 20th century fiction.

I have long complained that too much mediocre fiction is published, and so it is, and no one minds less than I do when some novel sinks back into the oblivion out of which it should never have been allowed to struggle. And no one regrets more than I do the consignment to that same oblivion of a number of very, very good novels each year.

I have a number of them on my own bookshelves, and a long list in my head. One of my dreams is to be given a free choice and plenty of financial support by some enterprising publisher, so that I could put a selection of my favourites into print again. One day, too, I shall compile a list such as the one produced by the late Cyril Connolly, of my 100 best post-war novels . . . though 500 would be nearer a sensible number.

A place would certainly be assured to a novel that seemed to me when it was published, 12 years ago, a modest masterpiece . . . *The Smaller Sky*, by John Wain. I re-read it last week, and I see no reason to alter my opinion of it. It is not a perfect novel – what is? – and in one or two minor respects it now seems a little dated, which doesn't really matter. It is an intensely moving book, a sort of realistic allegory. I would call it a poet's novel if I could be sure that the phrase carried much meaning. But certainly John Wain is also a poet, and there is something about the shape of *The Smaller Sky* and its balance and its imagery and the beauty of its descriptions which make me stick to the adjective poetic.

Superficially it is a quiet, low-keyed book, yet it is really a passionate plea for individual freedom and a cry of rage at the conventions, restrictions and insensitivities of certain human institutions. John Wain was not one of the so-called 'angry young men' of the 1950's for nothing. But I defy the most suspicious, hidebound and restrained of readers not to feel a heartbeat of response to the plight of its hero, Arthur Geary.

Geary has been a middle-aged commuter, conscientious, weary, supporting wife and family dutifully, successful enough, apparently contented. Then he begins to hear drums beating frenziedly inside his head, and he escapes, to live a life of perfect order and calm, on Paddington station, within whose confines alone he cannot hear the drums. He is totally law-abiding, has saved money to send regularly to his family, only wants to save his sanity. If you like, he is 'doing his own thing'. But should he? For the sake of his reason, and his children, his job, nice home and secure future, shouldn't someone 'rescue' him?

Various neighbours, friends, colleagues, experts, make the attempt. None of them deflect Geary from his purpose, or worry him seriously. But his relationship with his young son is a different matter. I have rarely read such an utterly convincing, honest and sensitive account of the deep, inarticulate, agonised love of a father for his young boy, in this case the brave, confused, lonely David.

'Something seemed to break inside Geary. It was as if, inside his chest, he had been carrying his feelings in carefully contrived glass containers. Now the containers shattered and his chest was flooded with blood, mush and broken glass. He opened his mouth to say something, but the possibilities jammed his brain. He wanted to say that he would leave the station and come home with David then and there. He wanted to invite David to move into the hotel with him. He wanted to explain to David about the drums. He wanted to promise David that he would leave the station hotel within a week and find a place to live where David could come and stay in every school holiday. Beyond all these things he wanted to say something that would lift the cold weight from David's heart and from his own. Nothing came and he allowed his mouth to close, drooping at the corners. Father and son looked at each other across the impersonal furniture.'

Alas, so far as I have been able to discover, *The Smaller Sky* is out of print in both its hard and paperback versions, but there may well be copies in second-hand shops, and on the shelves of libraries. It is so very good, that it is worth any amount of searching for but it is exactly the kind of novel that so easily sinks without trace, where other brasher, inferior titles get a lot of fuss and attention, and, even worse, a lot of reprints.

(1979)

P. G. Wodehouse

One evening during the recent holiday I was feeling particularly frayed at the edges, what with the festivities, Jessica's bad-tempered convalescence from German measles and those lowering, wet, early-dark days at the fag-end of the year. Only one remedy, naturally, so I retired early to bed with a hot toddy and a volume by one of those authors whose value is more than rubies, because they are guaranteed to tide – nay, lift me buoyantly and with a singing heart – over just such combinations of circumstances.

Which volume? It scarcely matters, my hand reaches to the three long shelves packed with his titles and falls where it will, and I take down whatever book it chances to be, certain to be content. And to be diverted, delighted, transported to another altogether more charming world, where the sun sets golden over rolling vistas of rose gardens, parks and messuages and the sweet birds sing, where all is lightness and frivolity and boyish pranks, and young hearts are sundered, but reunited in springtime, tribulations are resolved in an ultimate harmony akin to that at the end of Shakespeare's happy comedies; where the jokes are hilarious, comic situations rich, characters widely diverse and all of a kind with whom one would want to pass at least some of the time, if not actually to accompany on a walking tour of Scotland . . .

But I promised myself that I would not get carried away. For I have learned from bitter experience that there is simply no use my waxing lyrical about this author, when half the world, amazingly enough, simply cannot stand him at any price, or see what I'm getting at and why the fun. The other half, of course, consists of true believers. But it is not to fellow afficionados of P. G. Wodehouse that I am addressing myself.

We shall have to get together sometime to trip the light

fantastic and play favourite quotations from Jeeves, and set quizzes beginning: 'How many pig men did Lord Emsworth employ to look after the Empress of Blandings? Give Christian as well as surnames, and order of appearance'. No, that is a secret and private language, the language of love, which to the uninitiated outsider sounds like the babble of idiots and just as boring.

It may not be possible to convert those detractors of Wodehouse, and the baffled and uncomprehending, to full membership of the fan club – though I should dearly love to think that, as a result of my enthusiastic promotional efforts, one or two of you gave *Summer Lightning* or *Stiff Upper Lip, Jeeves* another try, and found that the door had clicked open and illumination dawned, so that you romped through them with enjoyment and laughed and saw the point at last. That would be reward indeed. But, as I myself know well in relation to, say, Scott and Jane Austen and Arthur Ransome, it is perfectly possible to admire and respect a writer, to agree that they are good and to know why, without actually caring for them very much or wishing to spend time in reading and re-reading their work.

It ought to be possible for anyone interested in the art and craft of story telling, in the history of humour, and in English prose writing, to appreciate why P. G. Wodehouse is a master, a genius of inventiveness and versatility, brilliant in his use of language, more adroit than almost any novelist since Dickens at working out a complex package of plot, sub-plot, and sub-sub-plot.

If you cannot stand Bertie Wooster's chinless idiocy, the turn-of-the-century upper-class code and behaviour, all the silliness of bread-throwing at the Drones Club and the what-ho'ing and I-say-ing, do not care for Jeeves's oiliness, or the snobberies and unrealities of life at Blandings Castle – well, I can sympathise, even though I love them all. But an open-minded reading of one of the most flawless books – say, of my absolute favourite, *The Mating Season* – ought to give rise to deep admiration of the style, pacing and plotting, careful construction, and wide and immaculately employed vocabulary, on the part of even the most curmudgeonly, and dull would he be of soul who could get through the King's Deverill village concert party chapters without a chuckle, if not a few cracked ribs.

I would quote from that, about the terrible Kegley-Bassington family, who sing, recite, play violins and do rhythmic dances, and about Bertie's sinking heart as the time approaches when he is to recite 'Christopher Robin goes hoppity-hoppity-hop', knowing that the rustic standees at the back of the hall are growing increasingly restless; but it is probably unfair to wrest even some of those little chunks of purest gold out of their total setting. For Wodehouse is all of a piece, his art is seamless and the whole fabric, plot, characters, set-pieces, language, humour, cross-references, atmosphere, meshes most beautifully together, varying subtly in pace and mood, so that the reader is kept alert and amazed, amused and admiring, as the book progresses.

Evelyn Waugh said: 'Mr Wodehouse's idyllic world can never stale' and it is true, and it is all an idyll, the Blandings books are perfect English pastoral; of course it is all fantasy, for our delight, we can immerse ourselves in it and forget, be refreshed and soothed and delighted, and curiously enough, the effect is also a strengthening and lasting one. I always emerge from my time with Wodehouse feeling happier and more carefree, less irritable and more relaxed, convinced that the real world cannot be so bad as I had feared, and able to see life a bit more steadily and whole, and to put its minor irritations and inconveniences into perspective again.

That is the sort of thing all great art does for us, among other things. I would go so far as to call Wodehouse great minor art, and that is not to devalue it, only to set it in a wider context. Even those who genuinely, and after much trying, cannot themselves get a taste for Wodehouse, must agree that there cannot be much wrong with a writer who has that magical effect upon so many.

(1980)

Rebecca

by Daphne du Maurier

I recently spent four pleasant evenings watching the repeat of the BBC Television serial *Rebecca*, and thinking how good it was, and how exactly right. The casting was perfect – the girl, Max, Mrs Danvers, were as I had always imagined them, yet somehow better – and that house, Manderley, one of the most famous of all houses in literature – this *was* Manderley.

As usually happens after I have seen or listened to the dramatisation of a novel, I went straight back to the book, and reread it at a sitting. I hadn't opened it for over twenty years, and I had thought I remembered it well, but of course I didn't, there were only certain scenes, vivid in the mind, odd snatches of conversation, a loose outline of the plot, and that unforgettable opening sentence, 'Last night I dreamed I went to Manderley again'.

Now television adaptations, even if they are not especially good ones, do the original novelist a service precisely because they introduce his work, via the screen, to a huge new audience, but I do not know which is better from a reader's point of view, the introduction to a new book, or re-discovery of an old favourite. In the case of *Rebecca*, apart from the sheer enjoyment of reading it again, the most important experience was a confirmation of what I had always suspected, that it is a far better novel than most people give it credit for.

Who am I to defend Daphne du Maurier? She has always sold far and away more copies of her novels than most contemporary writers; she is read, loved and remembered by millions; she was a bestseller in the days when the word still meant something – when bestsellers were real books by real writers, not packaged, artificial products put out by the international publishing machine to earn record sums of money, one-off titles entirely conceived with both eyes on the cash register.

Yet since *Rebecca* has been back in the public eye, I have heard the old phrases trotted out, the old, secondhand opinions given with an air of superiority and smugness. 'Light romance', 'Gothic melodrama', 'Pastiche of Jane Eyre', and Miss du Maurier is dismissed as 'popular', 'superficial', a writer of filmable stories full of cliché situations and hammy characters, the darling of the circulating libraries and, horror of horrors, 'middlebrow'.

I am not going to make out a case for her as a better writer than Charlotte Brontë, or as a great creative artist of the stature of Tolstoy and Dickens, as a maligned or neglected genius. I only want to protest about the injustice of the sneers of dismissal, to show that she is not only a very, very good, gripping, original storyteller, and that much of the criticism levelled against her comes too easily to the lips of those who have either never read her books, or are relying on old and leaky memories, and clips from Hitchcock films.

The plot of *Rebecca* is unlikely, melodramatic, incredible, strained; so is the situation of the heroine; various happenings are lurid in the extreme – Gothic, indeed. What gauche, naive little companion would ever be proposed to by the rich, upper-class, older-gentleman, Maxim de Winter? Who can believe much in de Winter, the suave, sophisticated, worldly-wise hero with a terrible hidden secret, a shadowed past, a slight touch of cruelty? Their marriage, and the circumstances of their return to Manderley are pure fantasy, as is that of Cinderella and Prince Charming.

The whole revelation of how Rebecca really died, the near-tragedy saved in the nick of time by the London doctor's astounding information, the happy ending, the terrible fire . . . I don't believe in these for a moment. But then, I don't believe in those other great romantic heroes, Heathcliff and Mr Rochester, or the more urbane 'older man', Mr Knightley, who marries Jane Austen's Emma. I don't believe in many of Shakespeare's plots or in the mad wife in *Jane Eyre* – and read the proposal scene in *that* novel before curling your lip at Maxim de Winter's, 'I'm asking you to marry me, you little fool'. There may be a fire at Manderley, as there is at Thornfield Hall, but at least Maxim isn't blinded as well, Charlotte Brontë's final sentimental stroke.

I need not go on. The point is that plots by themselves don't matter, they are more often than not, even in great literature, contrived, unbelievable, melodramatic. You suspend disbelief in the plot of every single Iris Murdoch novel, as in three-quarters of her characters, yet few people dismiss her so lightly, or rate her so low, as they do Daphne du Maurier.

Apart from the fact that it is marvellously imagined, that there are some magnificent scenes and set-pieces, that much of the writing is as good as you will find in most 20th-century English fiction not created by a handful of geniuses – just read the opening chapter again – and that it is breathtakingly well-paced, there is a depth of emotion, a quiet wisdom about human experience and relationships, the understanding of a developing maturity, in *Rebecca*, which lies below the highly-charged and coloured surface, and gives it a seriousness of purpose, a reason for being, a lasting value and great richness.

Rebecca is about growth – the growing-up from the isolation, naivety, shyness and awkwardness of youth, into adulthood; the growth and ripening of love, the realisation of what happiness and contentment and riches truly are; it is about change and dawning self-awareness, about the calm after the storms of first passion, as well as about those storms themselves. It is also about evil, revenge, malice, and the torment those conditions cause to those who suffer them, and suffer under them. Great themes indeed, but they are not lightly, arbitrarily or vulgarly handled.

The novel deserves its place in our hearts because it is a great romance, and in our memories because it is graphic and haunting. It can and should be read the first time with bated breath. And then read again, more calmly and carefully, for its more significant, less obvious qualities.

(1980)

Back to Childhood

'You must spend such a lot of time reading', they say and yes, so I do, but nothing like as much as I did when I was a student, or a full-time reviewer. The reasons are manifold, and to do with the burgeoning of other interests and with domesticity – and, of course, with Jessica, now aged 3¼, though it won't be too long now before she and I will sit side by side reading our separate volumes, and then I shall be able to do some catching up.

But it's also thanks to her that I do a lot of one kind of reading – aloud – from a certain kind of book. I have always thought it a great pity that many people assume that children's books are only meant for children. They stop reading them at whatever age, and never go back, at least on their own behalf, as it were. But the best children's books can't be hived off and labelled 'For ages 5–12' – they can be enjoyed by adults; they were, after all *written* by adults.

I would be rather glad to spend a few weeks marooned in a lighthouse (cosier than a desert island, and the books would stay dry) with a selection of my favourite books for young readers of all ages. And perhaps there should be a few of the sort I never got along with when I was a child myself, for our tastes change and develop, there might be all sorts of unsuspected pleasures in store. I didn't care for animal books – so no *Just So Stories* or *Black Beauty*; nor for the sort of fantasy that verges on science fiction, about unreal countries with peculiar names, out of time and space; nor for the sailing-camping-exploring adventures of the school of Arthur Ransome.

The books would have all seemed to be flavoured in a particular way – they have, perhaps, a slightly old-fashioned air, though they are not historical. I really must reread E.

Nesbit's books again, especially those about the Bastable family and that delightfully gritty book, *The Family from One End Street*. Then there's *The Secret Garden*, of course, and Mary Norton's books about *The Borrowers*. I didn't encounter those tiny people who live hidden away in our houses until I was well into my twenties, and I loved them at once. The same is true of the work of Leon Garfield and Penelope Lively and Joan Aiken, for example, and my enjoyment and admiration for their work is unreserved, not merely that suspect sort which smacks of sentimentality and nostalgia for lost youth.

The few titles I have mentioned out of hundreds of choices, are classics of their kind, and of course, as a child, I adored many books of little or no literary merit, but which catered well for my transitory passions – ponies, acting, ballet, medicine, boarding school. I have sometimes tried to reread *Angela in the 5th* or *Bella, Ballet star*, or *Penny's New Pony*, and failed to get beyond the first chapter. No matter, they served their purpose.

I wonder if my daughter will find a later return to her current favourites at all rewarding? Night after night, her father and I have to choose between a story in the series by Dorothy Edwards about *My Naughty Little Sister*, or one of Joyce Lankester Brisley's tales of *Milly Molly Mandy*; Beatrix Potter, Dick Bruna, A. A. Milne and *The Elephant and the Bad Baby* have all fallen, (I hope temporarily), from grace.

The favourite stories are all about small girls, with whose personalities, lives, families, homes, Jessica seems to identify eagerly, for all they are very so different. Dorothy Edwards's volumes of stories were first broadcast on *Listen with Mother* and I have read them to numerous children over the past ten or twelve years. Milly Molly Mandy was created in the 1920s, and was dated even by the time I came to read the stories during the war. That doesn't seem to trouble Jessica.

They both appeal because they both have utterly distinctive flavours, and tremendous character. *My Naughty Little Sister* has an elder sister, who tells the stories, a friend who lives nearby, called Bad Harry, and any number of adult cronies, ranging from kind, sweet Mrs Cocoa Jones who lives next door, to workmen mending the road, window-cleaners, postmen, Mr Blakey the shoemender, and a very very old woman in an old people's home.

The strength of the books, indeed, lies in the nature of these relationships, which are exactly what many children, including my own daughter, *do* have; but above all, in the personality of the heroine. She might be called headstrong or wilful, she has a mind of her own, great independence, resourcefulness and nerve, flair, and calculating, captivating charm.

Which is more than can be said for Milly Molly Mandy, a prim, wishy-washy little girl in a striped cotton frock, who lives with Mother, and Father and Grandpa and Grandma and Aunty and Uncle, and runs errands and is obedient and contented and altogether the opposite of my naughty little daughter. Yet Jessica loves the stories about her, and goes through our own village imagining that *here* is the nice white cottage with the thatched roof where they all live, and *here* is Billy Blunt's father's corn shop and Miss Muggins's general stores and little-friend-Susan's house and the blacksmith's forge . . .

I think my own affection for the books *is* purely nostalgic – I can remember how I felt when first hearing them – and they describe a way of English country life that is gone, and for which we may long. But that doesn't explain Jessica's identification with them. Perhaps it is just that they are plain, simple, wholesome and small-scale enough for her to accept?

Still, the relationship between any child and a favourite story which feeds its imagination is a very strange and unaccountable thing. In that way, too, there's no difference between then and later.

(1980)

Women Writing

At the back of my mind, like stones carried along by a stream, there are always certain questions. I take them up from time to time, worry at them, half solve them, perhaps, and put them back. Some are of tremendous importance, matters of life and death, others merely intriguing trivialities.

One that I have lately been prompted to take a fresh look at concerns women and the novel. Do women have a particular kind of imagination or creative personality that finds expression particularly in the novel form? Is there such a thing as the female imagination, or, indeed, as 'the novelist' in any sense deeper than 'one who writes novels'? Is it merely practical considerations which have made more women novelists than composers or painters? Is the novel a feminine art form?

I have been stirred into speculation this time by sight of a pile of novels and a catalogue that arrived on my desk lately from that enterprising, and, to some, off-puttingly named, publishing house, Virago Press. Besides books of an overtly feminist nature, both fiction and non-fiction, with which I am not here concerned, it produces an excellent paperback series, handsomely presented, called Virago Modern Classics, reprints of novels by women writers whose names may or may not be familiar, but whose individual titles have long been unobtainable, though not deservedly so.

They are the products of an enormous range and variety of talent, and I cannot commend them too warmly, but I note in passing that they are not only by, but largely about, women, though not in any narrow sense. So what, you may say, half the great novels of the world, and certainly, in England, written by women, have heroines rather than heroes, their individual social and imaginative worlds are presented through women's eyes. Isn't that inevitable? Women simply know more about women, than about men.

Practically speaking, and even at one artistic level, I would agree. In a domestic, sexual, experimental sense, of course they do. But what I am discussing is the creative sensibility of the novelist. Is there such a thing at all? Do women possess it more often than men? If you have it in you to be a creative artist, is it merely chance and circumstance that sends you in the direction of novel-writing – if you had had environmental stimulus and specialist training, might you not equally well have been a painter or a composer? Why have women written so many fine novels (as well as so many thousands of mediocre, or plain bad, ones)? Why do they continue to do so? Why do women read novels more than men?

Huge questions, perhaps only loosely related to each other, too, and whole books have been written in an attempt to answer them. I cannot be dogmatic, but I shall let loose a few hares, and hope to return to chase some of them up in the future. The first thing to note is that several of my hares go in completely opposite directions.

Small girls prefer fiction. Boys like facts from their books. I would have doubted the truth of that enormous statement until I had a daughter, and simultaneously became aware of, and interested in, the tastes of friends' children, boys and girls. Of course some boys like stories, some girls like encyclopaedias of astronomy, but time and again I see fiction being preferred, intuitively understood and responded to on the deepest and most subtle level, by the girls, and being rejected, uncomprehendingly, by the boys. The preference has nothing to do with intelligence or mere subject matter, and seems to be established from the beginning. When boys do grow to like fiction, they prefer it to be, as it were, full of fact.

Having sent off that particular hare, I turn to the nature of the novelist. Only a small proportion of those who write and publish novels, even competent ones, can be called true novelists, but I have no doubt that there is such a particular kind of person, with a very special kind of imaginative drive and specific talents and intuitions. Practical, circumstantial considerations apart, they are no more likely to have become painters or composers than Olympic athletes. The true novelist has a gift which has been bestowed by the angels, is born as well as made, is that one kind of creative artist and no other.

Moreover, I am certain now that this gift or talent is absolutely sexless. A great creative writer is, for the purposes of his art, neither male nor female. The woman novelist may write about women, their sensibilities and situations, or she may not, but one of the essential marks of the true novelist is the uncanny ability to take the imaginative leap, to get under the skin and into the shoes of any other person at all, as different from the writer as may be, in sex as in anything else. There is something magical about this ability both to become other people, to enter fully into them and convince the reader of the imaginative truth of the resulting observations and insights and, at the very same time, to be totally detached, from outside of, above and beyond, all those characters. For detachment, the slightly odd sense of being a participant, but also a witness and recorder, is another of those distinctive marks of the true novelist.

So, at the highest and deepest levels, there is no differentiation, not even an acknowledgement of the existence, of sex. At other levels, sex has been one of the most important issues in the history of the novel, and women have turned the form to their particular creative purposes more than any other art, for good reason. The history of the greatest art is sexless; the history of the other arts at all levels below the very greatest, is largely masculine, but the history of the novel has been hugely influenced, and its course directed, by the female imagination. Exactly why and how far this is so will preoccupy me intermittently for the rest of my days.

(1980)

Rubbish

When I was a child, my mother greatly disapproved of my reading either books by Enid Blyton, or comics like *Beano* – indeed, she went so far as to attempt to ban them altogether. That, of course, is always a counter-productive move, since in the strong-minded and rebellious child, it merely encourages secretiveness, and a hot desire to read more and *more* of what has been forbidden, possibly to the exclusion of anything else.

I *did* read both Blyton and *Beano* surreptitiously, generally underneath bedclothes by torchlight; I went through the complete works of the former like an express train through a tunnel – and out at the other end. I found them, after a while, unsatisfying and I must have grown tired of their pedestrianism, plus the paucity of vocabulary, and lack of imaginative power (not that I recognised these things, of course, I merely grew out of, and bored with the stuff). But certainly, they did me no harm at all and, while they lasted, gave much innocent, escapist pleasure. (All literature is escapist – the point is, whether it is *only* that.)

My daughter has now discovered Enid Blyton and specifically, the 'Famous Five' and 'Secret Seven' books, and I haven't discouraged her enthusiasm. It certainly isn't exclusive and seems likely to be fairly short-lived.

She enjoys *Beano*, too, which doesn't seem to have changed since I was seven, but to exist in some wonderful time-warp, full of the same silly characters (likewise its fellow, *Dandy*) – the Bash Street Gang, Lord Snooty, Korky the Cat, Dennis the Menace. How innocent, and how utterly removed from both reality and fantasy. The delights of *Beano* are those of happy laughter; a general silliness pervades all. It's hard, now, to understand why my own mother disapproved. I think she had such astonishingly high aspirations for me.

I find the same attitude – though it is almost entirely intellectual, rather than social – in evidence among some of the parents of my daughter's contemporaries. Enid Blyton isn't so feared now, because she isn't so universally popular, and because, by the side of some of the rubbish available, her books seem rather good, not to say innocent and slightly dated. I haven't discussed *Beano* and *Dandy* but I do detect a climate of opinion which feels that it is fine to buy your children illustrated papers if they are full of useful facts and helpful in connection with academic prospects. (By the same token, it's OK to watch Blue Peter but not Mighty Mouse.)

I haven't any patience with that Gradgrind sort of line. There ought to be a place for sheer, silly, harmless, pointless rubbish in anyone's life.

But I'm not being entirely honest. The rubbish that is Blyton and *Beano* has a charm for me, and others of my generation – the charm of nostalgia. I know it isn't harmful, but the truth of the matter is that there is plenty of pulp around today of which I disapprove far more passionately and violently than my mother disapproved of Keyhole Kate. There are comics and books (and, of course, children's television programmes) I aim to steer Jessica clear of, at least until she is rather older, and although I feel that my reasons are sound ones, I am a little uneasy at my own intolerance.

When my daughter is fourteen or so, I shall tolerate the inevitable intrusion of the pop scene into our lives; I might enjoy some of it myself, but not yet; *Beano* and *Dandy* she can have, but not that host of teeny-bopper magazines aiming to thrust Boy George, and the rest of the tawdry pop sub-culture down the throats of 5–10 years olds.

Apart from the pre-teen pulp, the only other sort of rubbish that troubles me is what I can only call 'evil fantasy'. Now, I'm not a science fiction person, and when I was younger, other-world books left me cold. I can't read Tolkien, either. So anything about trolls, gnomes and other invented species goes under my heading of unreadable but I certainly don't disapprove of it, as a genre. Why should I? I hate oysters, but I wouldn't dream of thwarting my husband's passion for them.

But on the borders of fantasy and sci-fi lurk more sinister books, ostensibly to do with epic-heroic battles between other-worldly forces of good and evil, and very appealing to the kind of child who likes to play Dungeons and Dragons. Yet to me, they are not only badly written, violent, crude, they give off the reek of sulphur and seduce the innocent young into a fascination with the occult. They are books I would actually ban from the house, and if I found them, I should burn them.

But I'm getting carried away. At the moment, Jessica is into the *Jungle Book* and the *Mountain of Adventure*, and anything by the master story-teller Roald Dahl, and Roger the Dodger and Kenneth Grahame and, and, and . . . I don't think we've got much to worry about. Just so long as she doesn't want to start writing the things . . .

(1984)

Writers and Places

'The remarkable situation of the town, the principal street almost hurrying into the water, the walk to the Cobb, skirting round the pleasant little bay, which in the season is animated with bathing machines and company, the Cobb itself. . . with the very beautiful line of cliffs stretching out to the east of the town, are what the stranger's eye will seek; and a very strange stranger it must be who does not see charms in the immediate environs of Lyme to make him wish to know it better.'

And certainly, to make him wish he had known it in Jane Austen's day. Lyme Regis, in the gloriously warm, cloudless first week of September, was indeed 'animated with bathing machines and company', and with traffic, ice-cream vans, unruly children, the smell of chips, wasps and motor-boats. But take away a few superficial 20th-century trappings, a few buildings and signboards and you would have the place, and its situation, very much as Miss Austen had it.

Indeed, it doesn't take more than a day or so's work by the special effects department of a film company to help to restore the past, for they have 'artificially aged' the lower end of the main street for the filming of John Fowles's novel *The French Lieutenant's Woman*, and very pretty and convincing it is, too: I hope they keep it looking that way.

But we didn't go to Lyme because of Jane Austen, for I am not an Austen fan, very far from it. Nor did we go because of Mr Fowles, whose original, gripping and intriguing novels I greatly enjoy. Still, you can't altogether discount or escape the literary associations of a place if they're at all significant, and since our return I've been thinking about the whole subject of writers and places. And it's a vast subject, there is only room for some random observations here. If you want a fine, thoughtful and rich treatment of more of it, together with some magnificent photographs, there is Margaret Drabble's recent book, *A Writer's Britain: Landscape in Literature* (Thames and Hudson).

There are two main kinds of association a place may have with a writer. He or she may have lived there, perhaps been born and bred, perhaps established a famous house there. There may or may not be much of and about the place in the person's work, but somehow, the essential spirit of the writer, it is believed, must still pervade it.

So, we can visit Scott's Abbotsford, or Kipling's Batemans, Haworth Parsonage and the cottage where Thomas Hardy was born, Shakespeare's birthplace, and so on. Many do. They may be changed out of all recognition, like Stratford, or scarcely at all, like Haworth; they may be preserved, the 'atmosphere' somehow sealed in, along with the writer's desk and chair, books and pens.

I don't really know what people do get from visiting all these places – not often, I don't think, a deeper insight into the works. But it's a pleasant pastime, and gives point to a tour of the country.

There are other places, which exist, are real, can be explored, and yet do not exist at all, can never be known, except via the imagination. Hardy's Wessex, Wordsworth's Lakes, Lawrence Durrell's Alexandria, the moors of *Wuthering Heights*.

Of *course*, they are real places, even though the names may have been altered, the precise geography shifted about a bit. We can buy an explanatory guidebook, and map and walk about Wessex, can't we? And if the towns, Shaftesbury and Dorchester and Sturminster Newton and Weymouth, and the innumerable tiny villages, have all changed in our century, the downs and barrows, fields and woods and hedgerows, are still there, though sometimes under a different state of agricultural cultivation. But there, nevertheless, little different. Every summer, thousands of earnest Japanese tramp about, for Thomas Hardy is mysteriously popular in that country. And Americans go to the glens of Robert Burns, and all manner of people ramble in scrupulously guided parties through 'Dickens's London'.

Why? Because when people love literature, they want to get right inside it, live in it, be there at that time with those people in those places, and one of the ways they imagine they can do it is by visiting the settings. I know what they seek. They will never, ever, find it. They will arrive and look and a gradual chill of disappointment will creep over them. They will wander and wonder, sometimes in realisation, sometimes in bewilderment, and go again, no nearer. What they seek, like the end of the rainbow, eludes them and always will.

For these 'real places' are no more than artificial façades, like those artificial shopfronts at Lyme. They are merely signs of maps, hints and whispers, beckoning fingers, beckoning the visitors on, towards the books. Hardy's Wessex, Wordsworth's Lakes and Beatrix Potter's Lakes, Emily Brontë's Yorkshire Moors, these are landscapes of the mind, places of the imagination, based, it is true, upon the real and visible, but bearing the same relation to it as the fleshly body to the soul and spirit of a man. Perhaps less.

The places which lie at the heart of great literature (and which are more than mere backgrounds, or the scene of incidental happenings in the books), are re-created afresh by every reader, for himself. That is part of the share he takes in the making of the work, that is why it is always a two-way process, and why the writer is only ever the partial creator.

Those named places are delightful to visit but when you are in them you will be as far from being 'in' the novel or poem as you always are – until you open the book and are in the middle of its pages.

(1980)

John Buchan

The greatest works of literature are sexless – that is, they transcend mere sexual differences. Tolstoy, Dostoievsky, Balzac, Dickens, their novels are read and understood by men and women equally. But on all the rungs of fiction below the topmost, there are, as well as novels that appeal to both sexes, those which very definitely are preferred by male or female readers – though not, of course, exclusively. And this is not any intention of the authors, either, for all authors write, not for men or women, but for themselves.

When we arrive at what I shall call, in the best Graham Greene-ian sense, entertainment literature, there is very decidedly a sexual divide; Greene himself is read by both sexes, but most pure adventure stories are preferred by men.

So, although I like to read for entertainment, as well as more serious purposes, I rarely read the very masculine adventure books. It is partly that the *macho* activities of their typical hero do not interest or excite me, and partly because, for the most part, these books are so very badly written, in ugly, brutish language and short, blunt sentences that bang your sensibilities over the head and numb them; they have no *style*.

But need that necessarily be so? I have spent the past week in the company of one of the masters of them all, and discovered, as I would have expected, that it need not; that marvellously evocative and accurate descriptive writing, elegance of expression, simple, clear use of language, can indeed go hand in hand with stories of physical exploits and derring-do travel, excitement, danger, violence, mystery, the thrills of the flight and the pursuit.

I have been reading John Buchan.

I began to do so for several reasons. I discovered by chance that Penguin Books have recently re-issued several of his books, and bought a handful in a pleasing little Cotswold bookshop. I then remembered that I had bought a couple of others at a bazaar last Christmas, for five pence each, and not yet got round to reading them. But a reason lay even nearer to home. The village in which I now live is in Buchan country. About these fields and in these woods and across the mysterious tract of land called Otmoor, Buchan used to walk; he lived in the Manor House of the village next-door, past which I drive almost every day – he was created Baron Tweedsmuir in 1935, and took the title of the village, Elsfield: he is buried in the churchyard there.

I recalled how greatly I had enjoyed the only Buchan story I had previously read, when I was only 13 or so, the most famous of all – *The Thirty-Nine Steps*. So, through a week of October cold wind and heavy rain, I had a marvellous orgy of Buchan. I read *The Three Hostages*, *Greenmantle*, *The Island of Sheep* and *Mr Standfast* – all Richard Hannay adventures, and one about that dry, dour Scottish lawyer, Edward Leithen, called *The Dancing Floor*. It is not well known and I don't think it is in print, but it certainly deserves to be; indeed, it would also make a splendid film. It is eerie, exciting and unusual.

Buchan is a master at the art of beginning a book, raising at once the pulse of his reader, and making him quite unable to resist reading furiously on. Things always begin quietly enough, perhaps in the peaceful English countryside on a clear winter's day, after Hannay has been out shooting, or by his fireside, after a good meal; he is relishing his rural retirement, when a telegram arrives, or an unexpected visitor arrives urgently . . .

From there, he takes us just about anywhere – to the South African veldt, or the wilder parts of Eastern Europe during the First World War, to the East, to Scotland; often, his hero is in disguise, and travelling uncomfortably and dangerously (and romantically) by cold night steam train or dirty tug boat up the Volga. For example in *The Dancing Floor* he travels in an old boat through storms, with a crew of hired mercenaries, to an idyllic Greek island – but arrives there not in glorious sunshine but in terrifying, sinister fog.

But he is as good at creating an atmosphere of fear, danger

and tension in London as in Istanbul. Greene puts it well in an essay on Buchan, written in 1947.

'John Buchan was the first to realise the extraordinary dramatic value of adventure in familiar surroundings happening to unadventurous men . . . Who will forget the first thrill in 1916 as the hunted Leithen, the future Solicitor General, ran like a thief in a London thoroughfare on a June afternoon?'

I am at once reminded, reading that, of the pursuit of the young man called Pinky through the civilised Regency resort of *Brighton Rock*. Greene learned the art of making the dramatic adventure happen in familiar surroundings to unadventurous people as, later, did John le Carré.

Graham Greene has also often written about how deeply he was influenced in boyhood by adventure stories but although he calls some of his works 'entertainments' I feel he always has a more serious purpose, which is absent from John Buchan's work, though there are certain traditions, rules of conduct and moral values heavily under-scored there. His view of the First World War does not accord with mine, and there are some objectionable racist turns of phrase here and there. But as novels of adventure his have not been bettered and they transcend the sex-barriers, to appeal to any reader who likes *his* or *her* entertainment reading to possess real literary merit.

(1981)

O-Level English

'She's just begun her O level English course', a friend told me recently, of her fifteen-year-old daughter, 'but I very much disapprove of some of her set books. They don't seem to study proper literature any more'.

I questioned her more closely, to try to discover what she meant by 'proper literature', of the kind suitable for examination syllabuses. She meant 'the classics' – novels, plays, poetry, written in past centuries, by writers whose names we had always been taught to revere, without completely understanding why. They might be called difficult books, too, with long sentences and some archaic language and preferably, I gathered, quite a few thee's and thou's. This, she implied, was 'real' literature, these are books which teach you something, not books to be enjoyed.

It all made me feel extremely depressed, as much on behalf of the dead authors as anything else. Did Shakespeare, Chaucer, Byron and Keats, Dickens, Hardy and George Eliot, write to be studied, dissected and paraphrased? Were they hoping to 'teach the reader something' – not in the best and broadest sense, for of course every creative writer hopes that his readers may learn something, albeit indirectly from his work – but to 'teach' pupils about narrative technique, vocabulary and the art of character depiction?

Did they think of themselves as classics? Would they want to be read not in the armchair but at the schooldesk and to be understood only with the aid of teacher's comments and editorial notes? How would they feel about being not literature but set texts?

Put like that, it sounds ludicrous, yet, unhappily, that is more or less what lies behind my friend's view of what constitutes the proper study of English literature for O and A level.

Now, I am certainly for the study, as well as the reading and enjoyment, of English, as of any other, literature, as an aid to the greater and deeper understanding and appreciation of particular books, and in order that the young reader may learn discrimination and discernment.

Inspired teaching of literature, even within the narrow confines of the examination syllabus, can and should lead pupils on to real enjoyment of a life-long and life-enhancing kind, and study of the subject can also be a useful tool for the cultivation of the arts of clear and careful thinking and self-expression, and of the critical and philosophical faculties latent in everyone.

Clearly, many of the authors we call classic are great writers whose work has stood the test of time and which is also resilient enough to withstand detailed analysis, at various levels, by those answering examination questions.

When young people become bored and alienated by books, the fault lies not in the books themselves but in the way they have been introduced and taught. Sometimes, in the past, examination set books were hangovers from the taste and judgement of another era, no longer of interest or relevance to today, nor of any intrinsic literary merit. Their cover has been blown but those who set the texts have not always realised the fact.

I also feel very strongly that some of the books which have often featured on the lists are too difficult for the young, in the sense of being too adult, too inaccessible in both style and content, for them to appreciate until they are far older, more mature and experienced in life and judgement. The books will not reveal their greatness after any amount of close classroom study, nor will they be read with any degree of pleasure, they will merely become boring, and so will remain closed in those later years when they might have yielded up their secrets.

The very best books, of course, can be read several times in the course of one's life, and appreciated at a new level each time. The very worst will be exhausted at a first, cursory reading.

I don't believe we should simply pander to what the young

think they want to study, any more than we are right to let a small child choose its own diet, but I do believe we should be very sensitive to their needs. The books they study should be both good literature, *and* enjoyable and relevant to them, their experience and abilities. Certainly, the only books on the syllabuses should never be books from the past. Literature is nothing if not a living subject, and there are a good many 20th century, and even living writers, worthy of attention.

I have recently been looking at a list of this year's set English literature texts from various examination boards, and, on the whole, I was favourably impressed, though I have to declare an interest – my own work appears from time to time. The past is well represented; there is always Shakespeare, and there are also Chaucer, Dickens, Hardy, Byron, Trollope, George Eliot. There are some of the best modern poets, but not enough of the best, yet more obscure, from previous centuries. Some old contemporary favourites continue to appear – *Cider with Rosie*, *To Kill a Mocking-Bird*, though they seem to be giving *Lord of the Flies* a rest at last, and it is good to see Graham Greene, represented not by one of the most obvious titles, but by *The Human Factor*.

Is there anything downright mediocre and unworthy of serious attention, even at Ordinary level? Yes, there are one or two pretty bad plays, though all are interestingly representative of their periods and have been popular in performance. I hope that teachers will be able to lead their pupils on to discovering exactly why and how they *are* poor and that they do not fall into the trap of believing that if it's on the syllabus it must be good.

Not many of the thousands who take these examinations will go on to study literature at university level, but I should like to hope that between us – writers, teachers, examiners – very many are set on the right road to a lifetime of enjoyment and enrichment from the world of books. Otherwise, the acquisition of the certificate is a fairly irrelevant achievement.

(1985)

Writing a Book

Whenever I have been persuaded, which is rarely, to talk in public about being a writer, I have been struck by the frequency with which the same questions are asked me. What people mostly ask is either 'Where do you get your inspiration?', to which the only two possible replies are either 'I don't know' or 'Everywhere', or else a question about the practical physical business of actually putting all those words on paper until a book is produced.

Most people are fascinated by the details of where I write and when and for how long and how much per day and with pen or typewriter. Actually, this all suits me very well, simply because I greatly dislike talking about the content of my own books, except in the most general way, but I will happily tell anyone all this sort of thing. And I am always curious to discover the writing habits of others, living and dead.

The whole subject has been in my mind recently because I am writing another book. I have not written one for seven years and it is a very strange, very nice feeling. I had rather forgotten, indeed, that it is what I have always most enjoyed doing and it is interesting how easily I have slipped back into the old familiar ways and habits as into a pair of well-worn shoes.

I have, of course, scarcely stopped writing just everything other than books. I only took two months off from this column when Jessica was born and if you had known her as a baby you would understand how proud I am of that! I have written radio plays, reviews, introductions to new editions of other people's books, journalism, television dramatisations of my own stories, you name it, and really it has all been hugely enjoyable and interesting. I like variety. I haven't the sticking power to spend five years or more of my life on a single, long project; my boredom threshold is too low and I dare say that is a great fault of character, but there it is.

How my husband happily spends his whole life with the man Jessica calls Mr Shakespeare I shall never understand. I have always written my novels very fast indeed because I can only keep the necessary white-hot interest going for a limited period.

But after seven years, I was beginning to miss the satisfaction that only book-writing can bring. All these short sprints are fine but the yearning to do the marathon again has been growing, I long to feel a solid, hard-cover in my hands, see my name on a new dust-jacket, sneak around bookshops in dark glasses and a false beard, propping my title up in a prominent position. Oh yes, and there is a bit more to it than that, I have something of book length to say again.

Now the one I am writing is not a novel. Oh-ho no. I have done with novels, I gave them up seven years ago and I have absolutely no intention of returning to them, and no more desire to do so than I have of smoking a cigarette again. Prose fiction of any kind is a chapter of my life closed, as it were, for all manner of reasons I won't go into here. My book is a work of non-fiction, though there is a good deal of what you might call invention going into it, but its subject matter has nothing to do with the way it is being written, and where and for how long each day.

Shaw wrote in a hut at the bottom of his garden at Ayot St Lawrence, and Virginia Woolf in a summer house in Sussex. Roald Dahl has a shed in Buckinghamshire, and I daresay there are many more writers at the bottom of gardens. I was lucky enough to have a similar eyrie myself for a couple of years but mostly I have used a room in the house.

So long as it is empty and silent, I do not much mind its other features, but it must be a room with a view, the more spectacular the better, though Patrick White has to have a blank wall before him, and so did Proust. In between pages I simply must have visual refreshment.

Tolstoy wrote in the morning when, as he put it, 'one's head is particularly fresh', and so have most others, though Dostoievsky wrote at night. Virginia Woolf did 250 words on a good day, and Trollope set himself by his watch to do 250 words every 15 minutes. I average about three thousand words in a working morning of four hours, and always have, not because that is what I demand of myself, but because it just falls out that way. I am interested to note that it still does, in non-fiction as in novel writing. I work in long hand, on lined paper, using biro, but I suspect that I am a dying breed, for every single other writer I know, apart from Angus Wilson, uses a typewriter. I could not stand the racket, and I can't type fast enough. Angus Wilson is also the only one I know of who writes outside in the fresh air whenever possible, wearing ear plugs always and an overcoat when necessary. I could never do that, because the sun or the wind or insects disturb the paper.

The degree of exhaustion at the end of a working morning varies, not according to the number of words produced but the creative emotional energy expended. Novel-writing was very tiring for me. My new book is not. I press steadily on, enjoying it as I go and finish feeling, as the essay for the school outing puts it, tired but happy.

I like the sight of my pile of paper as it grows a bit higher each day and I am greatly looking forward to writing 'The End', and then to seeing the book in print, first in proof then in its final binding, and to smelling that richly evocative smell of new book and to wandering into those bookshops, heavily disguised. Really, I must do this more often.

(1981)

John Betjeman

The other day, I came upon a photograph of my elder daughter, standing beside the grave of the poet John Betjeman, and I thought again how very glad I was to have taken it, and glad that she had been there.

I do not think that, at the age of seven, she understood very much about who he was. She may not, at the moment, even recall much about the day the photograph was taken either, but when she looks at it in later years, and, I hope, begins to read his poetry for herself, perhaps a dim memory of it will come back.

For it was indeed a memorable day, in September, sunny and windy and very clear. As we walked across the golf links to the small, tucked-away church of St Enodoc, we could see for miles, across the flat fields to the sea, under a wide, wide sky, and the friends who took us there told the story, most dramatic to a child, of how the stranded church had for some years been quite buried under sand, and then recovered.

We watched the golfers across the green, and brushed against late wild flowers, sending up clouds of butterflies, and I remembered bits of the poem he wrote about it all, 'Sunday Afternoon at St Enodoc Church, Cornwall' and my daughter jumped and danced about.

And then, there was the church, down a slight slope, and near the gate, the grave, roped around and topped by a simple, temporary wooden cross, and still filled with flowers, though they were fading, for it was only a week or so old. Because of his so-recent death, and the beauty of the place, and of the weather, I had expected more pilgrims, but there was no one else at all.

And as I stood, looking down at the grave, I thought a great many thoughts about Sir John Betjeman, and about myself, my own life, and his influence and impact upon me, realising, perhaps for the first time, how tremendous it has been.

I thought of how obsessed he had always been by death; those lonely deaths of sad spinsters, in flats converted from once-grand houses in spa towns of fading gentility; and by speculation about his own death – how it would come, and what would, or would not, come after it. He was a serious man, but not, somehow, a depressing or a pessimistic one, for all his questioning.

Reading the obituaries, and some of the best poems, of Philip Larkin, I was struck by quite the opposite thought – that here had been a deeply depressed and gloomy man, who saw no hope, finally, for any of us. But Betjeman's poetry, as well as his personality, had a much more lightening effect. It has made me happy. Yet there have been times when he has spoken to me at the deepest and most moving level I know. One of his poems had rung through my head constantly, only a few weeks previously, when I had sat by the side of my dying infant.

> Oh, little body, do not die.
> You hold the soul that talks to me
> Although our conversation be
> As wordless as the windy sky.

And now, here *he* was, buried, in this peaceful, beautiful spot, and all seemed somehow resolved, it felt absolutely right and good.

I thought gratefully of the many places he had opened my eyes to over the years, that tremendous, passionate sense he had of the importance of the ordinary, as well as the extraordinary, corners of England, old churches, neglected graveyards, all these beaches, coves, moors, harbours, of North Cornwall, and so many more. He made me see, during my growing years, when taste is formed for life, that Victorian architecture was magnificent. It was a lesson he taught a whole generation.

Railways, musty churches, municipal statuary, seaside boarding houses, leafy London suburbs, public schools, cricket fields, Oxford colleges, old ladies in bathchairs, childhood sights, sounds, smells, feelings – he gave them all such significance. I cannot go on a Southern electric train without thinking of him, or down the Belbroughton Road in Oxford, 'where early springs the spray', or past the Albert Memorial or Marlborough College. Odd lines pop like jingles into my head.

> Up the ash tree climbs the ivy,
> Up the ivy climbs the sun

and 'Phone for the fish-knives, Norman', and 'Furnish'd and burnish'd by Aldershot sun'.

When my third child was born, a friend assumed I had named her from Betjeman and was shocked that I did not, in fact, know the reference. I looked it up and there she is, 'Clemency, the General's daughter'. I'm glad she is, albeit accidentally, a Betjeman girl.

By giving us so much of himself, so many intimate details of his own life, his childhood memories, his fears, loves, obsessions, beliefs, by being so utterly truthful, John Betjeman does far more than simply tell us those things. He helps us to see our own selves, to learn about our pasts, and the places and people in them, to reveal what is important about our own experiences.

That was why I took the photograph, in the hope that one day my daughters will know and love John Betjeman, and the importance of that place.

(1985)

The Diary of a Provincial Lady

by E. M. Delafield

I was beginning to wonder if it would ever happen. That row labelled My Favourite Books has been the same length year after year. I read widely, deeply, questingly but though much has taken my fancy in a mild sort of way, the enthusiasm has proved fleeting, the books have not had staying power.

I am not talking, as anyone who reads this column at all regularly will know, about the great and the good, but about those precious, special, idiosyncratic favourites, generally funny, which have been faithful companions through fair days and foul, on long journeys, during bouts of influenza, at times of stress and distress, the ones which never fail to divert and delight and which come up fresh each time. All of them seem to fall into the 'love or loathe category', and I won't repeat the list again, it's too well-worn.

The point is that I have known them all for years and there have been no new ones, with the exception of *Adrian Mole*, which gained an honorary place overnight and looks like being given full membership very shortly.

And now, here it is, the perfect newcomer, so wonderful, so sure, it has by-passed the probationary section altogether, and flown straight up to join the permanent strength. 'At last', my family say, with sighs of relief, 'at last, she's found something *different* to re-read and re-read and carry about with her and chortle at and quote little bits from.'

But what I simply cannot understand is, where has it been all my life? Why have they been keeping it from me? Why have I had to wait for its recent reprint as a Virago Modern Classic? I asked around and discovered no less than three so-called close friends who have been in on it for years. Their respective excuses were, 'Well, I assumed you *must* have known it – doesn't everyone?'

'If you must know, I kept it to myself in case you didn't see the point', and, rather mysteriously, 'Yes, well you know what you're like'.

The only forgivable reason of the three is (b). People grow defensive about the joys of their favourite books. The worst judgment they would fear to hear fall from my lips would be that most damning word – 'Silly'.

Oh, but how could *anyone* . . . of course it isn't silly, it is glorious, simply glorious, as Toad would say, richly humorous, gently ironic and acutely perceptive, one discovers new joys, new lines to laugh at, new paragraphs to learn by heart, at every turn. It is of its kind, quite flawless, and it is called *The Diary of a Provincial Lady*, by E. M. Delafield.

Originally, it appeared as a serial in what was, in the 1920s and '30s, a feminist magazine, the weekly *Time and Tide*, but although its author is firmly on the side of women, there is nothing remotely strident, militant or overtly propagandising about it. 'The provincial lady', whose name we never learn, writes a diary of simple, domestic events – trouble with the servants, encounters with the vicar's wife and the Lady of the Manor, events in the village community, relationships with her husband and two children.

Crises relate to her perpetual struggle to balance her bank and household accounts (and regular, furtive trips to 'pop' her great-aunt's diamond ring – 'am greeted as old friend by Plymouth pawnbroker, who says facetiously, "And what name will it be *this* time?"').

The hysteria of their French governess, the arrival of a kitten (expressly forbidden by husband) which is christened Helen Wills when found playing with an old tennis ball.

She is, in a bleak sort of way, reasonably happy with her lot, which was one common to thousands of middle-class married women between the wars, but she also has aspirations to become more than a provincial lady; she enters the weekly *Time and Tide* competition, and even visits an old school friend, who moves in London literary circles, all of which eventually lead to her writing and publishing a successful book

– and that leads to a broadening of her horizons to such an extent that the last volume in the series is called *The Provincial Lady in America*.

But like all sequels, and especially those which open out what has previously been a very small, closed world, none of the three successors to the original diary is a complete and seamless book, nor do these have its compressed, selective charm. The whole point about the provincial lady is that she *is* provincial. It is the daily round of local encounters, family frustrations and domestic upheavals, which has such a rich flavour, and is the source of the very funniest passages.

There are some vivid, entirely credible, characters: the vicar's wife, determined, bossy, voluble; the martyred, hypochondriac mother of a young-ish spinster daughter who dares to find a suitor; Mademoiselle ('Note: Extreme sensibility of the French sometimes makes them difficult to deal with'); Cook ('Cook says that unless I am willing to let her have the sweep, she cannot possibly be responsible for the stove').

It can certainly be read for its sociological and period interest, for it depicts a world long vanished, a class and condition of women who no longer exist; like all the best comic books, it is more than merely funny. The provincial lady has a shrewd eye and ear for human pomposity, self-deception, silliness, snobbery, yet although she can be sharp, she is never cruel, she does not belittle.

She presents a remarkably honest self-portrait, but would have been surprised to be called virtuous. Her touch is deft, her wit sparkling, she disarms totally. The set-pieces in the book are quite hilarious, and above all, perhaps because of its diary form, it can be read in snatches, once the whole pattern has been discerned.

(1985)